LEVEL ONE QUESTIONS

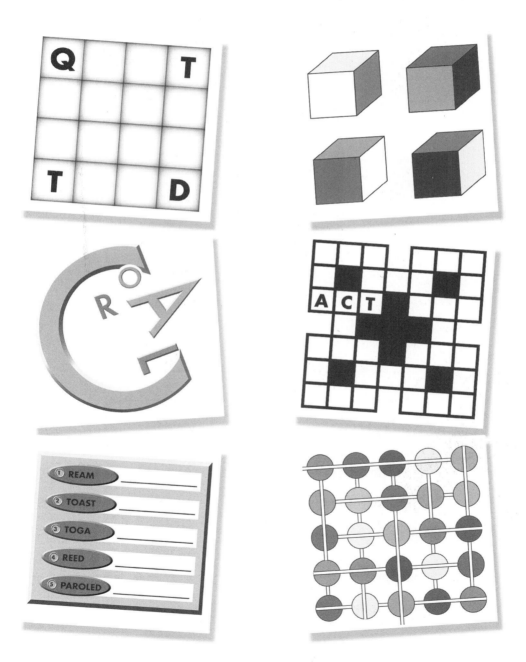

1. CUBED

Here are different views of the same cube. Each of the six sides has a different number. What number is the side that is opposite to number 5?

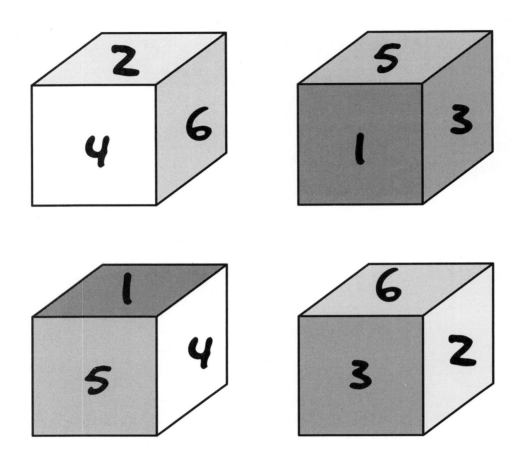

2. CLOTHES LINE

This line of ten letters can be split into two five-letter words which are the names of two items of clothing. Words read from left to right and the letters are in the correct order. What are they?

J E S A H I N R S T

_____ / _____

3. JIGSAW

Four toddlers have completed a jigsaw. Each child put one piece in place. From the clues, work out which piece each one put in and the order in which they inserted them.

- ○ The boys put in the bottom pieces.
  Neither of them put in the last piece.

- ○ Rosie's piece touches all the other pieces.

- ○ Danny's piece is not directly below Rosie's piece.

- ○ Tessa put her piece in place before Tim.

- ○ The bottom left corner piece was the first to go in place.

4. AFTER-WORDS

Which word can go after all these words to make new words?

C H E C K _____

K N O C K _____

P U L L _____

5. CREATURE CODE

In this code, shapes and signs have been used to take the place of letters of the alphabet. The first group makes ELEPHANT. Which creature is in code in the second group?

E L E P H A N T

6. CONNECTIONS

Find a route along the connections to get from the top left circle to the middle circle in the bottom row. The circular areas can spin around to allow you to connect them to another circuit, but you have to have landed on a circular area before that can happen.

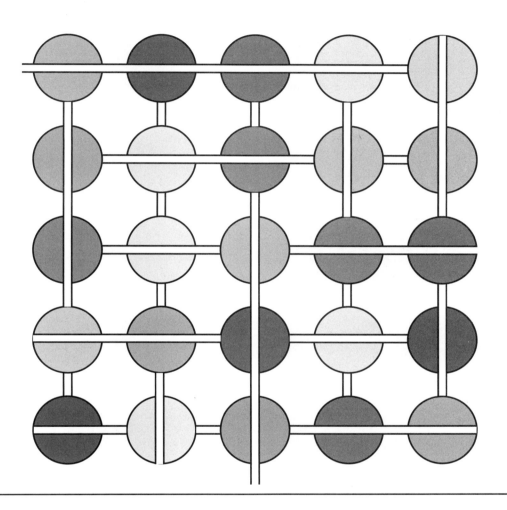

7. SECRET SEVEN

Rearrange the letters below to make a seven-letter word.

E L A P S E D

_ _ _ _ _ _ _

CLUE

Think HAPPY

8. TOP TEN

complete the word by filling the spaces with a whole number between one and ten.

1

6 4

T H R _ _ _

2 5

10 8 9 3

9. RUINED TEMPLE

Deep in the dense jungle lies the remains of the temple of the Werarwe people. For many years these brave, footsore souls wandered in the jungle crying out "Werarwe?" It is many centuries since they were lost forever, but the inscription on the ruined temple reveals that they tried to leave a message behind them. Can you work out what it meant?

10. LINKS

Which word will go after the first word and before the second word?

SHOPPING(_ _ _ _ _ _)BALL

11. BACK WORDS

Solve the clues: the second answer is the first answer written backwards.

TURN ROUND AND ROUND * PINCHES

_ _ _ _ * _ _ _ _

12. ADDER

Using other words with the same meaning, can you create
a new word from two separate ones?

NOT IN   _ _ _ _

+ WEEP   + _ _ _ _

= PROTEST   = _ _ _ _ _ _ _ _

13. ACT 3

With the word ACT in place, can you fit the words below containing three letters back into the frame?

ADD	BAT	CUE	EMU	ICE	SEA	YET
ALL	CAR	DIE	FEW	LIE	SOB	
AND	CRY	EAT	FUN	NOT	WET	

14. FRUIT SPLIT

The name of a fruit is hidden in the sentence below. Find it by joining words or parts of words together.

The sporting hero ran generously for charity.

_____

15. SPIKE LIKES...

- Spike likes peas but he hates spinach.
- Spike likes eyes but he hates ears.
- Spike likes ewes but he hates rams.
- Why does Spike like these things?

16. FACE FACTS

Use the letters that make up the face to make a name.

17. CRAZY CREATURES

Rearrange the letters in the words below to spell out the names of animals.

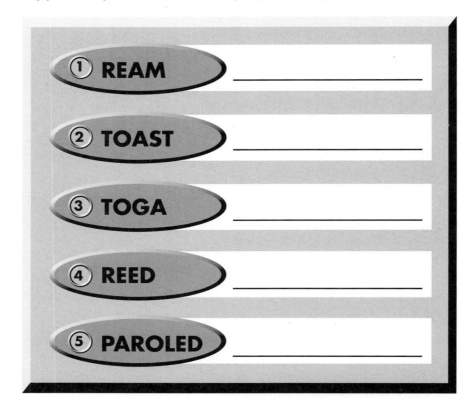

1. REAM _____

2. TOAST _____

3. TOGA _____

4. REED _____

5. PAROLED _____

18. GOING BATS

A word square reads the same across and down. Use the listed words to make two word squares. Each square must contain the word BATS.

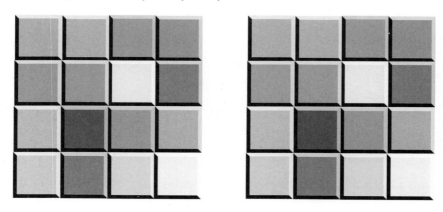

ACHE ARIA BATS BATS LAMB MIST SEND THEN

19. FLY THE FLAG

Each flag stands for a letter of the alphabet. The first group of flags stands for SPAIN. Using the same code, can you work out which capital city the second group of flags spells?

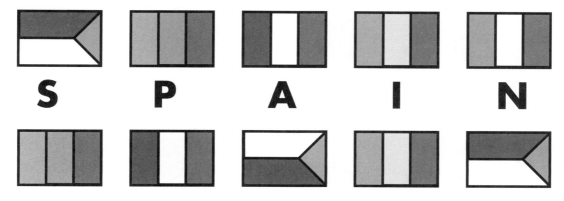

S   P   A   I   N

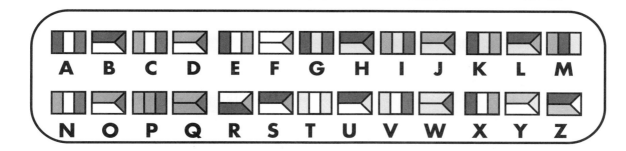

___   ___   ___   ___   ___

A B C D E F G H I J K L M
N O P Q R S T U V W X Y Z

20. SILHOUETTE

Which silhouette matches the outline shape?

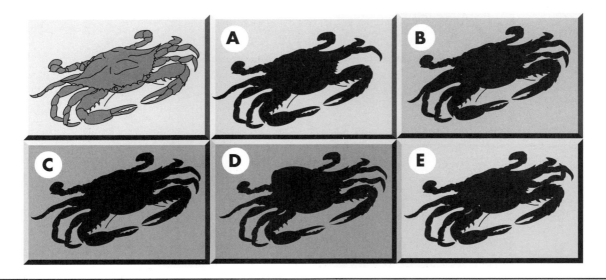

A
B
C
D
E

21. MIND THE GAP
Which single three-letter word completes all of the following words?

_ _ _ A T E

C A R _ _ _

P _ _ _ E C T

P A R _ _ _

22. COUNTER
How many triangles are there in this pattern?

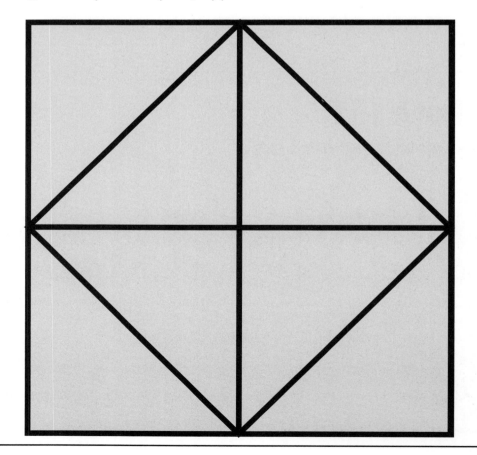

23. SECRET SEVEN

Rearrange the letters in the word below to make another word of seven letters.

U N P A S T E

_ _ _ _ _ _ _

CLUE

Think
SALTY SNACK

24. CAR CHASE

If the first group of shapes makes the word CAR, which moving item does the next group stand for?

C A R

_ _ _ _ _ _ _

25. WHAT'S NEXT?

what is the next letter to go in the space?

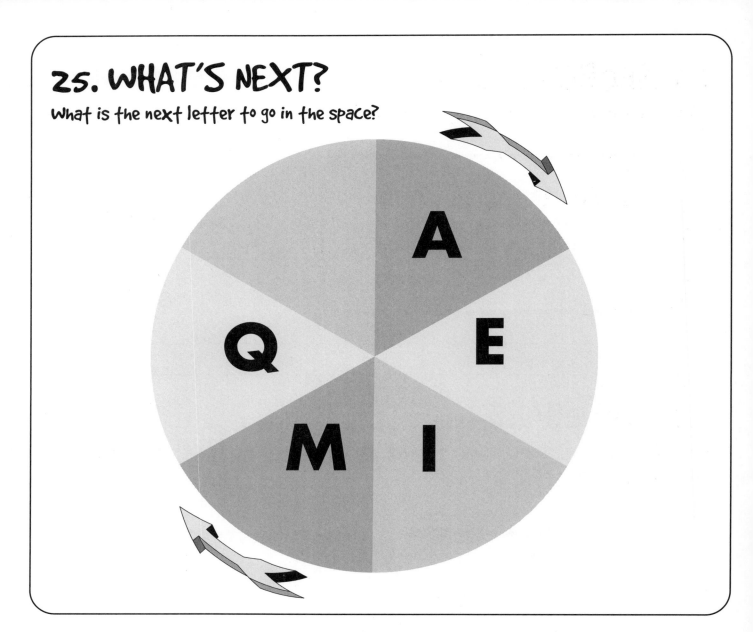

26. AFTER-WORDS

which word can go after all these words to make new words?

F L A S H _____

H O R S E _____

P A P E R _____

27. STARGAZER

All answers contain four letters and follow the direction shown by the arrows.

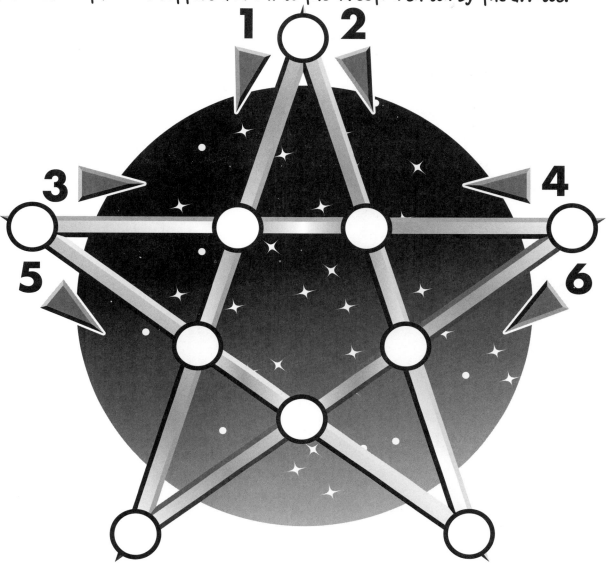

1. Very high
2. Ancient Greek city connected with Helen
3. Role in a play
4. A device to catch an animal
5. Cunning trick
6. Hammer, saw or spanner

28. NUMBER FIT

fit all the numbers back into the frame.

3 DIGITS

| 143 | 269 | 319 | 418 | 571 | 636 |
| 730 | 854 | 922 | | | |

4 DIGITS

1060	1139	2016	2873	3000	3227
4406	5891	6082	7030	7645	8107
9145	9543	9768	9844		

5 DIGITS

18341   24937   45780   80265

6 DIGITS

| 122259 | 201495 | 474934 | 546828 |
| 660571 | 752360 | 814073 | 939406 |

7 DIGITS

| 1039362 | 5852544 | 6676988 |
| 7486512 | 8557816 | 9963237 |

29. ON LINE

one line from each letter is missing. Can you fill the gaps to make another word for glue?

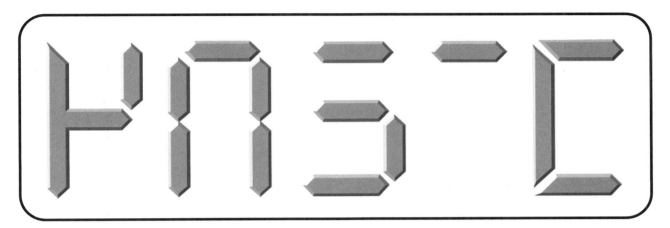

30. SECRET PLACES

The name of a country is hidden in each of the sentences below.
Find them by joining words or parts of words together.

1 We visited the spa in November.

2 That's the dress which I least like.

3 Can a date be decided upon for the party?

31. PATTERN PLAY
Find the remaining pattern from the given shapes.

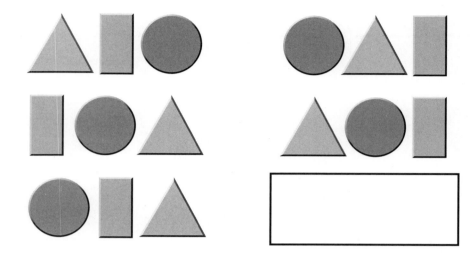

32. BACK WORDS
Solve the clues: the second answer is the first answer written backwards.

AMAZE   *   CASHEWS, PECANS, PISTACHIOS ETC

_ _ _ _ _   *   _ _ _ _ _

33. SPLITZER
This row of ten letters can be split into two five-letter words which are the names of two metals. Words read from left to right and the letters are in the correct order. What are they?

B S R A T S E S E L

/

34. MIDDLE MOVES

Each clue has two answers. Both answers are spelt the same except for the middle letter which is different.

1 Petroleum ✳ Wise bird

ANSWERS: _____

2 Lively dance ✳ Run gently for exercise

ANSWERS: _____

3 Fruit of a rose ✳ Leap on one leg

ANSWERS: _____

4 Worn with a tie ✳ Not very long

ANSWERS: _____

5 Sloping to one side ✳ Jumping up in the air

ANSWERS: _____

35. MORE OR LESS?

What is more, the number of hours in a week or the number of days in any six months?

_____

36. JUST JUICE

You are in a supermarket. Going down an aisle, the fruit juice is on your right.

You count ten different makes of fruit juice,

and there are ten cartons of each make.

You get to the end of the aisle, realise you have forgotten something and turn back.

This time looking to your left you see ten different makes of fruit juice, and there are ten cartons of each make. How many cartons of juice have you seen altogether?

37. WHAT AM I?

My first is in show
But isn't in son.

My second's in nor
But isn't in run.

My third is in rare
But isn't in sea.

My fourth is in reel
But isn't in tree.

My fifth is in ride,
But isn't in rise.

I'm the land where you stand
I'm the seas and the skies!

What am I?

38. NEWS ROUND

Solve each clue and write the answers into the spaces in the grid. All answers have four letters. Put the first letter in the outer circle, then move towards the centre. Only one letter changes between answers, and answer 8 will be only one letter different from answer 1.

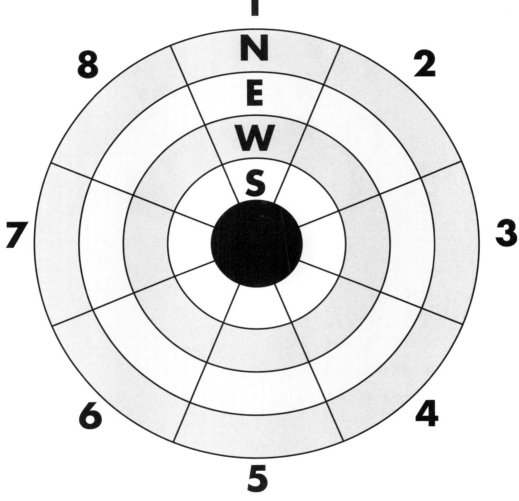

1. **Up to date information**
2. **Mesh in a hockey or football goal**
3. **Hamsters, cats and dogs can be these**
4. **Green vegetables**
5. **The sound of ringing of bells**
6. **Sea creature**
7. **Oceans**
8. **Uses needle and thread**

39. ALPHA-SEARCH

In this puzzle you have to search out the things that aren't there! Here's a jumble of letters of the alphabet. Each letter appears once, except for some letters which do not appear at all. First, work out the missing letters then arrange them to spell out the name of a fruit. You need to discover five letters.

Z F W R K N S
Y U X Q
T V
L O G M D J B I

40. NUMBER RING

Move around the circle. You have to write a number in the blank section that will continue the number pattern.

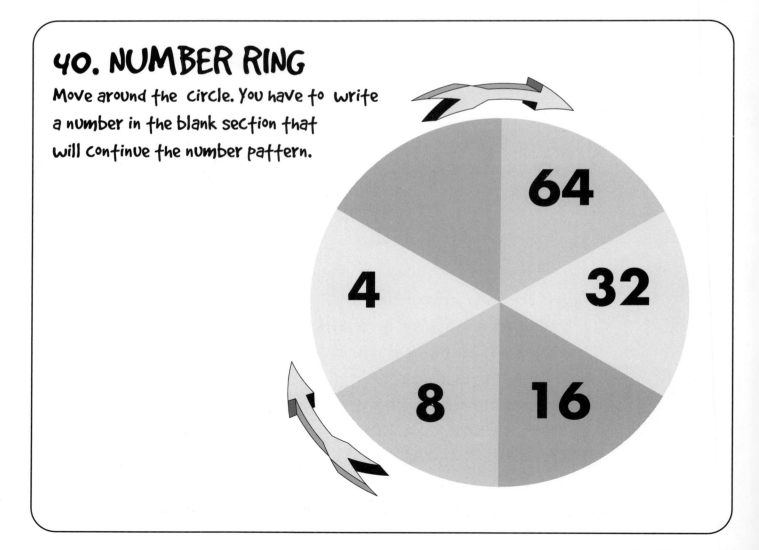

41. SALT SIGNS

Shapes and signs have been used to take the place of letters of the alphabet. Can you work out what the words are? They are all things that could be found on a dining table. The first word is SALT.

1

2

3

| S | A | L | T | | |

_____

_____

42. LINKS

Which word will go after the first word and before the second word?

N O R T H (_ _ _ _) V A U L T

43. BACK WORDS

Solve the clues: the second answer is the first answer written backwards.

DOMESTIC ANIMALS ✳ DANCE MOVEMENT

__ __ __ __ __ ✳ __ __ __ __ __

44. CORNERED

The corner letters are in place. Use all the listed letters to complete the grid and form a word square in which words will read both across and down.

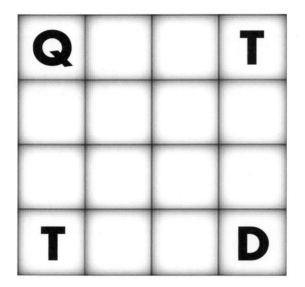

Q			T
T			D

A A D D E I
I N O O U U

45. FACE FACTS

Use the letters that make up the face to make a name.

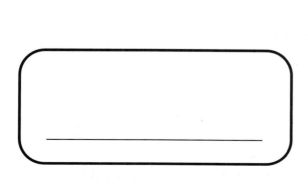

46. ADDER

Using other words with the same meaning, can you create a new word from two separate ones?

ISN'T   — — — —

+ FROZEN WATER +   — — — —

= POSTER   =   — — — — — —

47. SHAPE UP!

Can you unscramble the groups of letters to spell out the names of different shapes?

① CEON   _____

② BUEC   _____

③ RQUESA   _____

④ ICLERC   _____

⑤ ANRTILEG   _____

48. SECRET SEVEN

Rearrange the letters in the word below to make another word of seven letters.

P R O T E S T

_ _ _ _ _ _ _

CLUE

Think
CRAFTSMEN

49. STARTING BLOCKS

How many more blocks are needed to make the upper layer the same size and shape as the lower layer?

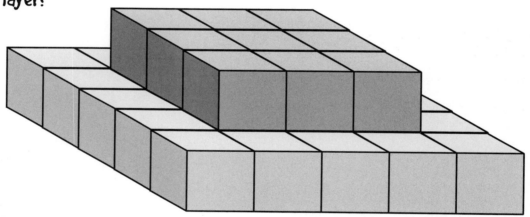

50. AFTER-WORDS

Which word can go after all these words to make new words?

P A S S _____

P U L L _____

W A L K _____

51. MIND THE GAP

Which single three-letter word completes all of the following words?

S _ _ _ A L S

H _ _ _ S O M E

V _ _ _ A L

S _ _ _ W I C H

52. CALL ME A CAB!

Fit the listed words into the grid to make four word squares, each containing four words. Each word square reads the same across and down. One word is in position to start you off.

DONE   NEED

EDEN   NEST

ENDS   OBOE

EXIT   OOZE

ITEM   PLUM

LOSE   SOON

MESS   TAXI

MITE   USES

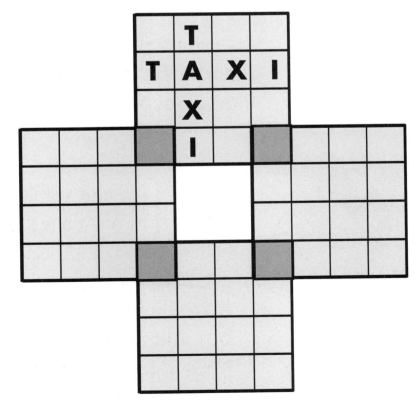

53. SECRET SEVEN

Rearrange the letters in the word below to make another word of seven letters.

R E P L A Y S

_ _ _ _ _ _ _

CLUE

Think HERB

54. NICE ICE

Can you work out the names of the four friends and say which ice cream flavour they like best?

1

Katie likes pistachio.

One of the boys likes chocolate.

2

3

I like vanilla. I'm not called Ben.

Liza likes orange but Alan doesn't.

4

55. IN THE BAG

You have five baseball hats in a carrier bag. You give each of your five friends a hat each and find that you're not left with an empty carrier bag. Why not?

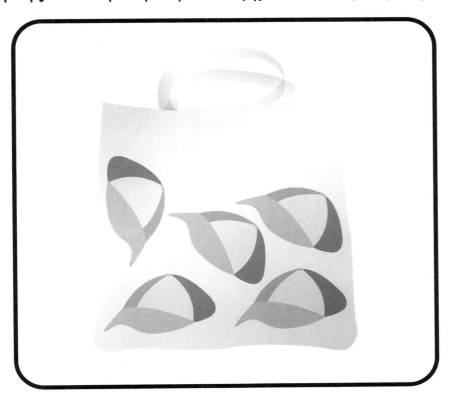

56. ADDER

Using other words with the same meaning, can you create a new word from two separate ones?

ARMED CONFLICT — — — —
+ OBSERVED + — — — — —
= POLISH CAPITAL = — — — — — —

57. FIGURE FACES

Each face is made up of numbers. When the individual numbers are added together which face gives the highest total?

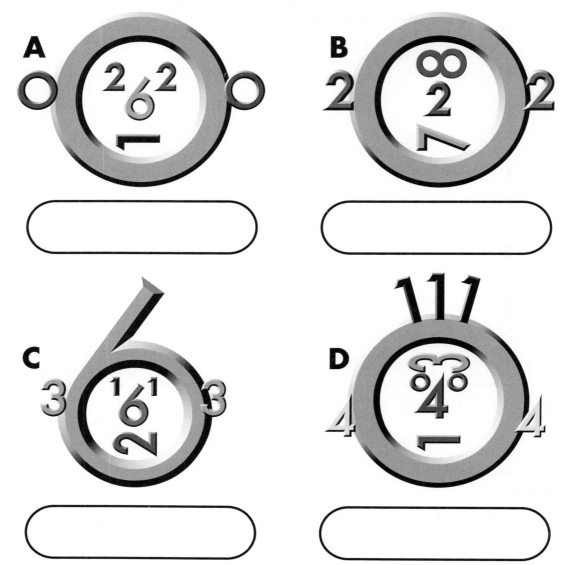

A

B

C

D

58. LINKS

Which word will go after the first word and before the second word?

LAMB(_ _ _ _)SUEY

59. SPLIT UP

The words below have been split in half and the ends moved around.
Can you repair the splits?

STAR	1	a	CAKE
SWIM	2	b	KNOT
SACK	3	c	SUIT
SIDE	4	d	RACE
SEED	5	e	FISH
SLIP	6	f	KICK

60. SECRET SEVEN

Rearrange the letters in the word below to make another word of seven letters.

PIRATES

_ _ _ _ _ _ _

CLUE

Think
CELEBRATIONS

61. TOP TEN

complete the word by filling the spaces with a whole number between one and ten.

6 4 **FOO _ _ _ RK** 2 5

62. DUNGEON DOOM

Find a way through the connected dungeon cells that will lead to escape!

START

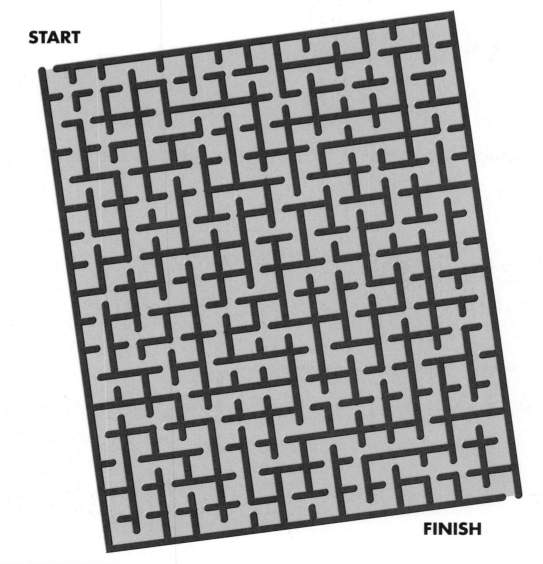

FINISH

63. AFTER-WORDS

Which word can go after all these words to make new words?

C H O P   _____

D R U M   _____

L I P   _____

64. YOUR DEAL

Using the listed words, make three word squares which read the same across and down. The word DEAL appears in each square.

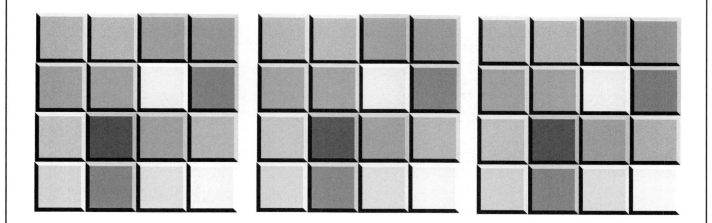

**ANNA ASKS DAZE DEAL DEAL
DEAL ELSE GLAD LESS LINE
ODDS SLEW**

65. ADDER

Using other words with the same meaning, can you create a new word from two separate ones?

FRIEND　　　　　— — — —

+ REALLY COOL　　+ — — —

= QUEEN'S HOME = — — — — — —

66. MIND THE GAP

Which single three-letter word completes all of the following words?

— — — S E

H I D — — —

G A R — — —

— — — T I S T

67. BOXED IN

Any group of four straight lines can make a rectangle. Using this as a guide, which shape appears in the most rectangles?

68. CAMOUFLAGE

The name of a wild animal is hidden in the sentence below. Find it by joining words or parts of words together.

The bridge will span the river when finished.

69. LINKS

Which word will go after the first word and before the second word?

S C R A P (_ _ _ _) M A R K

70. NAME GAME

Each face stands for a letter in the alphabet. The first group makes IRENE. The second group makes JAN. Which name is formed by the third group?

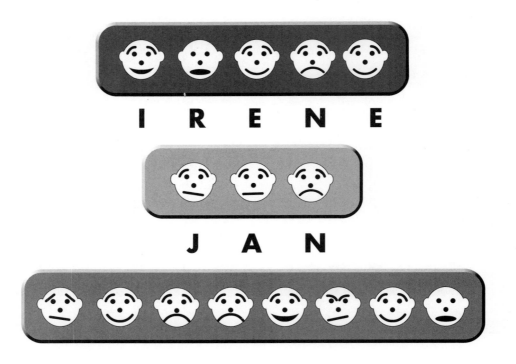

I R E N E

J A N

_ _ _ _ _ _ _ _

71. SPLITZER

This row of ten letters can be split into two five-letter words which are the names of two breeds of dog. Words read from left to right and the letters are in the correct order. What are they?

B O C O R X E R G I

/

_____

72. SHEEPISH

Which sheep is the odd one out?

73. BACK WORDS

Solve the clues: the second answer is the first answer written backwards.

DUTCH CHEESE   ✳   **CREATED**

✳ _ _ _ _   ✳   _ _ _ _

74. FRUITY

What type of fruit can you make out of 'one rag'?

75. METAL DETECTORS

The name of a metal is hidden in each of the sentences below. Find them by joining words or parts of words together.

1 I find my tonsil very painful despite all the treatment.

2 It was a big, old dog.

3 All the while a drain was overflowing.

4 It's just not fair on others.

5 He seems to have lost interest in everything.

76. WHAT'S NEXT?
What is the next number to go in the space?

31

28

31

30

31

77. TOP TEN
Complete the word by filling the spaces with a whole number between one and ten.

C A _ _ _ _ _

78. PYRAMID

Fit the words back into the pyramid grid. Each word is written in a mini-pyramid shape. The first letter of each word goes in a numbered space. The second letter goes in the space directly above, the third letter goes to the right and the fourth letter goes to the left. There's a one-letter start, but be warned there's only one solution!

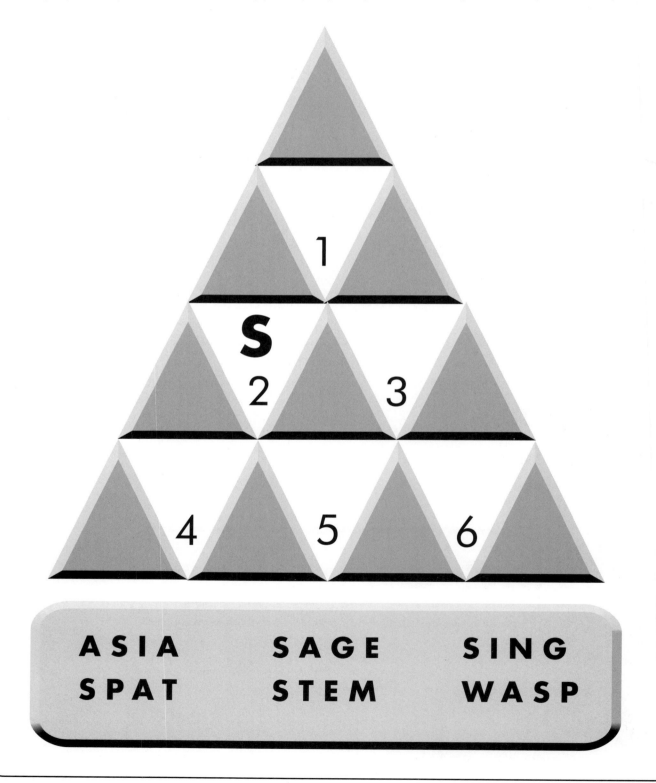

ASIA   SAGE   SING
SPAT   STEM   WASP

79. SECRET SEVEN

Rearrange the letters in the word below to make another word of seven letters.

E N T R A P S

_ _ _ _ _ _ _

CLUE

Think
RELATIVES

80. CDS

Donna collects CDs:

Pop CDs make up half
the collection.

Dance CDs are a quarter
of the collection.

Rock music CDs are an eighth
of the collection.

There are four CDs of movie
soundtrack music.

How many CDs are
there altogether?

81. LINKS

Which word will go after the first word and before the second word?

WATER(_ _ _ _)OUT

82. HAT TRICK

Which arrow has not gone through the cowboy hat?

83. AFTER-WORDS

Which word can go after all these words to make new words?

B A S S _____

E A R _____

K E T T L E _____

84. SQUARE SEARCH

A word square reads the same whether looked at going across or down. You need to find five words in the letter grid that can be used to form a word square. The first word has been found for you.

S	C	A	R	E
C				
A				
R				
E				

85. FRUIT CODE

Can you crack the following code and find four fruits? If PEACH is written as QFBDI and STRAWBERRY is written as TUSBXCFSSZ,
what are these?

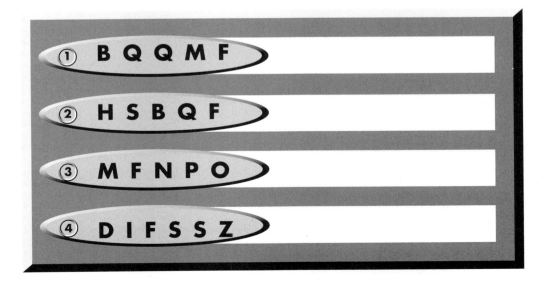

① B Q Q M F

② H S B Q F

③ M F N P O

④ D I F S S Z

86. NOW YOU SEE IT...
Can you decide what this number is from the small amount shown?

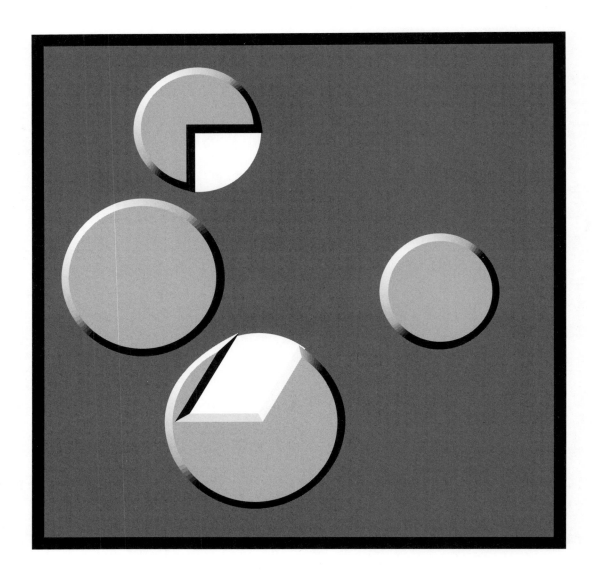

87. 'EAR' EAR
Lady Lotts has a jewellery box full of earrings. She just has two types, gold and silver. All the earrings are of the same size and pattern. She's in a rush dressing for dinner and, without looking, grabs a few earrings from the jewellery case. How many earrings would she need to have taken to be sure of picking up a matching pair?

88. NUMBER-RING

Move around the circle. You have to write a number in the blank section that will continue the number pattern.

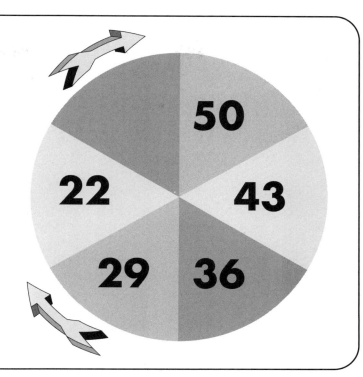

89. FACE FACTS

Use the letters that make up the face to make a name.

90. SPLITZER

This row of ten letters can be split into two five-letter words which are the names of two colours. Words read from left to right and the letters are in the correct order. What are they?

B E G R I E E G N E

/

91. VIDEO PLUS

Fit all the words back into the grid.

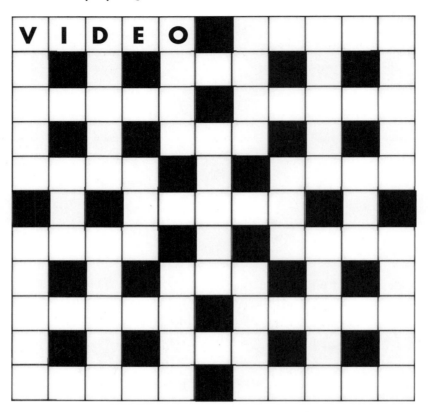

3 LETTERS

AGE	AIR	ASK	EVE
KIT	PAL	TRY	USE

4 LETTERS

ALPS	AMEN	AUNT	EVEN
KILT	OKRA	RELY	STAR

5 LETTERS

ALERT	CHARM	DIVAN	DRAIN
ICING	IDEAL	INGOT	KITES
LEVER	LLAMA	NOTES	RACED
REINS	SLICK	TONGS	VEGAN
VILLA			

92. BACK WORDS

Solve the clues: the second answer is the first answer written backwards.

SWALLOW GREEDILY * **ELECTRIC SOCKET**

___ ___ ___ ___ ___ * ___ ___ ___ ___ ___

93. CLOCK OUT

Which of the clocks in the box below could logically be placed as F?

A

B

C

D

E

F

94. SECRET SEVEN

Rearrange the letters in the word below to make another word of seven letters.

S T A P L E R

_ _ _ _ _ _ _

CLUE

Think WALL COVERINGS

95. LINE UP

Which line is longer - A or B?

A

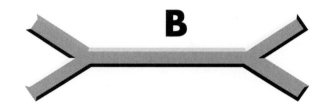

B

96. MIND THE GAP

Which single three-letter word completes all of the following words?

_ _ _ **E A R**

F R I _ _ _

D E F _ _ _ **E R**

S P _ _ _

97. ADDER

Using other words with the same meaning, can you create a new word from two separate ones?

GREEN VEGETABLE — — —

+ DIRECTED + _ _ _

= **MAKES A SOUND LIKE BELLS** = — — — — — —

98. WINNING TICKET

From the information given, match each child to their ticket and decide which prize each one won.

99. AFTER-WORDS
Which word can go after all these words to make new words?

BOILED _____

EASTER _____

POACHED _____

100. ON TARGET
Which three numbers on the target must be hit to score exactly 100 points?

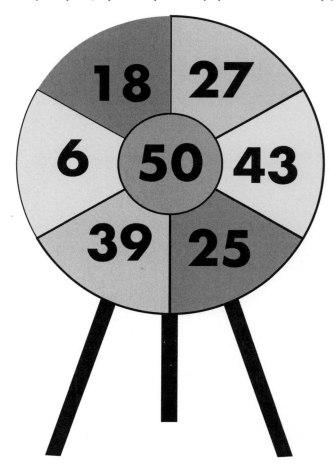

101. MOSAIC

Fit the letter tiles back into the frame. When the tiles fit together in the right order, the mosaic has five words reading across, and four words reading down.

102. SPLITZER

This row of ten letters can be split into two five-letter words which are the names of two drinks. Words read from left to right and the letters are in the correct order. What are they?

C O W A C O T A E R

/
_____

103. STACK SYSTEM

As you work down the stack, remove a letter from your answer to get the next answer. Once you've reached answer four, you then add a letter each time until you reach the bottom of the stack. You can change the order of the letters if you need to.

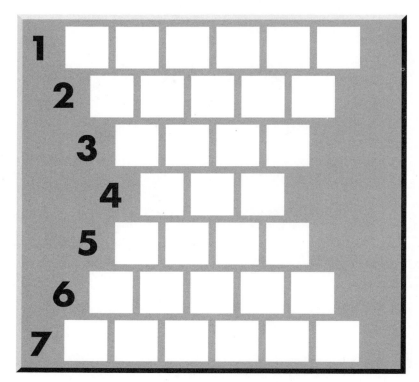

1. Painter
2. Begin
3. Major movie or TV performer
4. Long tailed rodent
5. Rip
6. Our planet
7. Dad

104. LINKS

Which word will go after the first word and before the second word?

H E R B (_ _ _ _ _ _) P E A S

105. DIFFERENT DIGITS

Travel downwards from number to number along the links to reach the bottom digit without having repeated a number.

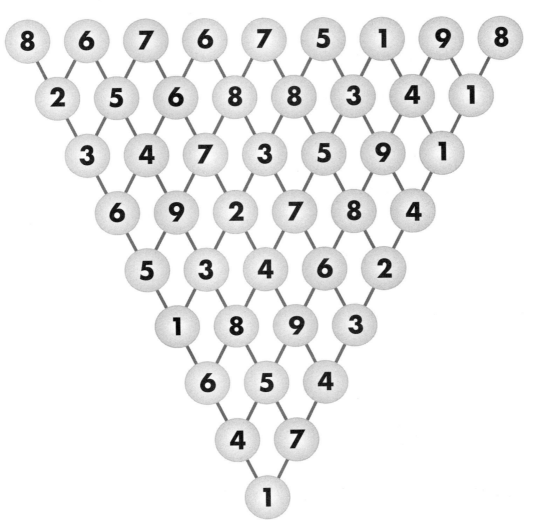

106. SECRET SEVEN

Rearrange the letters in the word below to make another word of seven letters.

S E C T I O N

_ _ _ _ _ _ _

CLUE

Think POSTERS

107. CATNAP

Can you unscramble the groups of letters to spell out places where animals sleep?

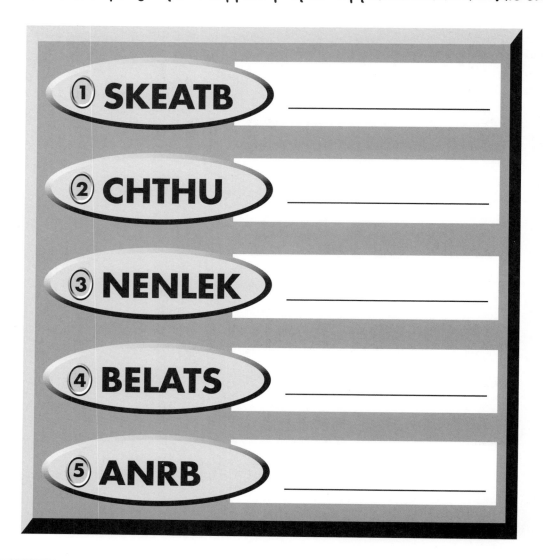

① SKEATB _____

② CHTHU _____

③ NENLEK _____

④ BELATS _____

⑤ ANRB _____

108. BACK WORDS

Solve the clues: the second answer is the first answer written backwards.

HARD WORKING STUDENT * **PULLS ALONG**

___ ___ ___ ___ ___   *   ___ ___ ___ ___ ___

109. MIND THE GAP

Which single four-letter word completes all of the following words?

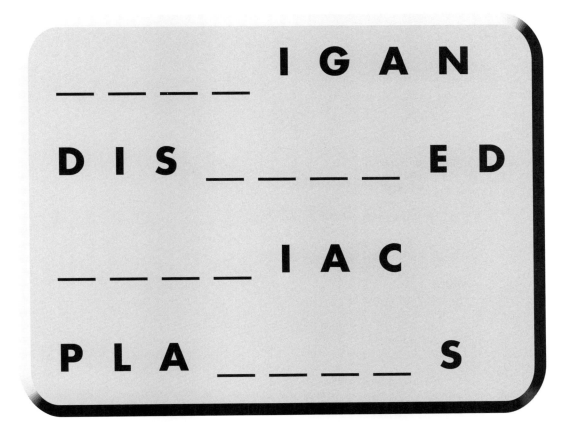

_ _ _ _ I G A N

D I S _ _ _ _ E D

_ _ _ _ I A C

P L A _ _ _ _ S

110. ADDER

Using other words with the same meaning, can you create a new word from two separate ones?

COOKING UTENSIL — — — —

+ HAVE A GO   + _ _ _ _

= FOOD STORAGE
CUPBOARD

 = _ _ _ _ _ _

111. NUMBER-RING

Move around the circle. You have to write a number in the blank section that will continue the number pattern.

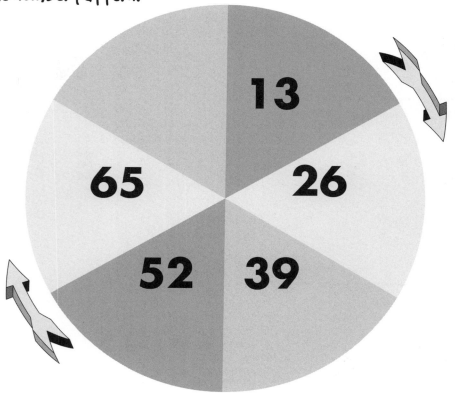

112. AWAY DAY

Laura looks at words upside down.

Miriam reads words backwards.

Niall reads words from left to right, as most of us do.

There's a word about a time of the day which reads the same to all three friends. The word is written in capital letters. What is it?

113. WHEELIES

One of the tracks below doesn't match any of the wheels shown. Which is it?

114. FRUIT SPLIT

The name of a fruit is hidden in the sentence below. Find it by joining words or parts of words together.

'To show appreciation, clap please at the end of the performance.'

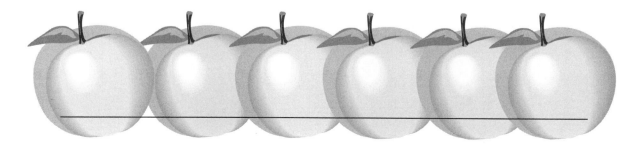

115. TAKE SIDES
Which group has most sides?

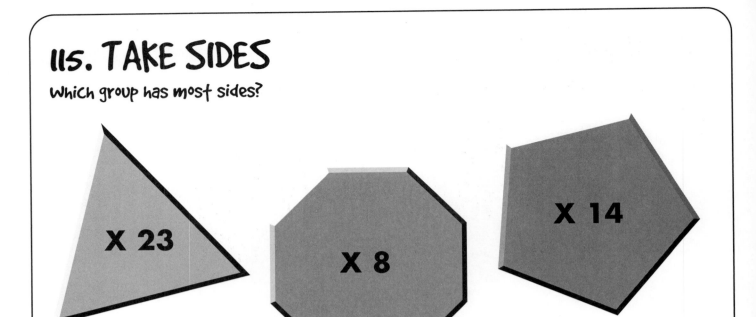

X 23

X 8

X 14

116. LINKS
Which word will go after the first word and before the second word?

D O G (_ _ _ _ _ _) M A I D

117. AFTER-WORDS
Which word can go after all these words to make new words?

BRASS _____

RUBBER _____

STEEL _____

118. STARTING BLOCKS

Fit the nine blocks back into the grid to make a crossword in which words read either across or down and link together. The first word across is something linked with thunder. The first word reading down is something used to cut the grass.

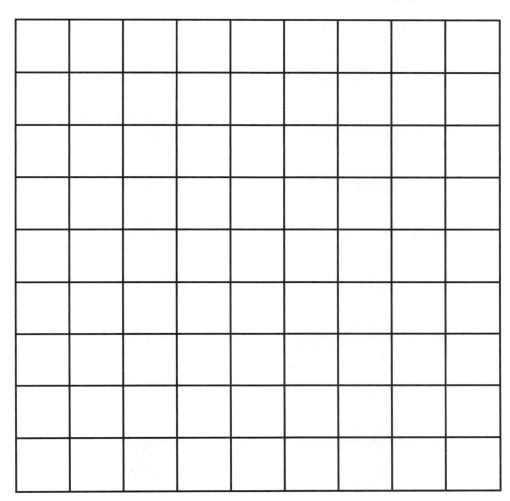

119. SUM SHAPE

In this sum, shapes have taken the place of numbers. Can you work out the numbers that the shapes have replaced?

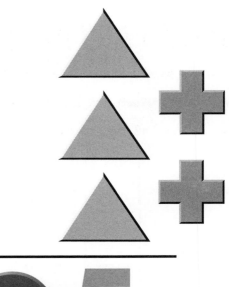

120. MUSIC BOX

Use every letter in the box to name a musical instrument.

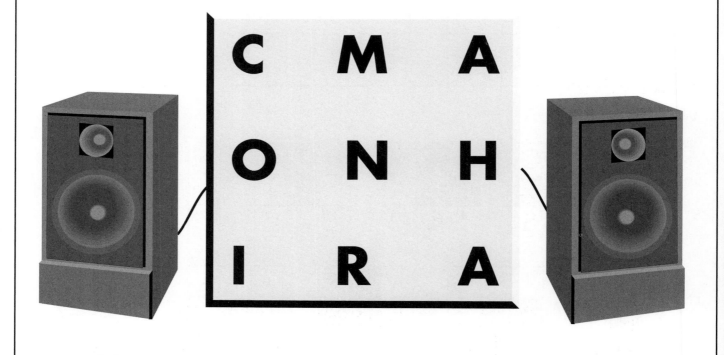

121. S.O.S.

Solve the clues and write the answers into the frame. Each answer contains an SoS.

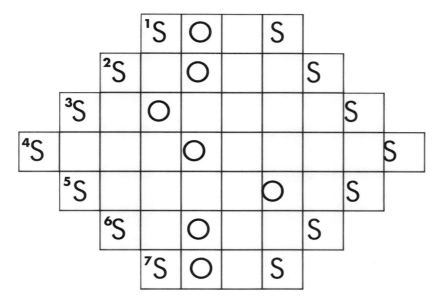

	¹S	O		S		
	²S		O		S	
³S		O			S	
⁴S			O			S
⁵S				O		S
⁶S		O		S		
	⁷S	O		S		

CLUES
1 Cries **2** Yells **3** Free from dirt
4 Followers of a sporting team **5** Paper cutters
6 Trousers for the summer **7** Male children

122. WHAT'S NEXT?

What is the next letter to
go in the space?

Z
X
V
T
R

123. CROSS PURPOSES

Four of these pieces can fit together to make a cross shape, like the one shown. Which piece is not needed?

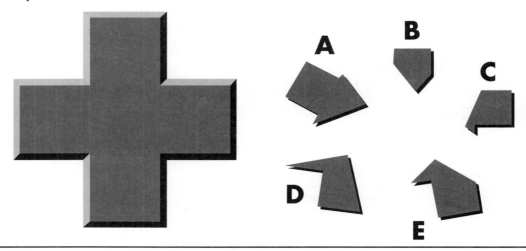

A
B
C
D
E

124. RHYMER

My first is in meat
But isn't in late.

My second's in hot
But isn't in hate.

My third is in lunch
But isn't in chain.

My fourth is in sale
But isn't in lane.

My fifth is in lame,
But isn't in lamb.

Use all the letters
To spell out what I am.

125. MORE OR LESS?

Which is greater – the number of letters in half an alphabet, or the number of times the small hand of a clock goes on to five within a week?

---

126. MIND THE GAP

Which single three-letter word completes all of the following words?

___ ___ ___ **C H**

A R ___ ___ ___ **G E**

F ___ ___ ___ **C E**

B ___ ___ ___ **D**

---

127. BACK WORDS

Solve the clues: the second answer is the first answer written backwards.

STOLEN GOODS * UTENSIL, PIECE OF EQUIPMENT

___ ___ ___ ___ ___ * ___ ___ ___ ___ ___

128. TWINS

Which two faces are exactly alike?

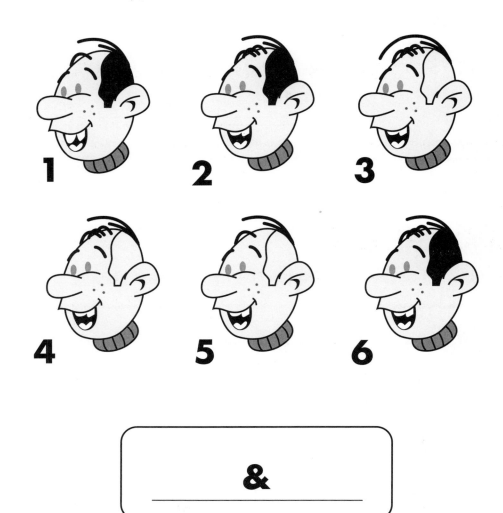

&
_____

129. COMPU COMMAND

Add one line to complete each letter and spell out a computer command.

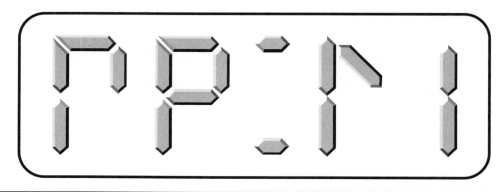

130. SECRET SEVEN

Rearrange the letters in the word below to make another word of seven letters.

D E S C E N T

_ _ _ _ _ _ _

CLUE

Think PERFUMED

131. POINTED

Are there more arrows pointing up, or are there more arrows pointing down?

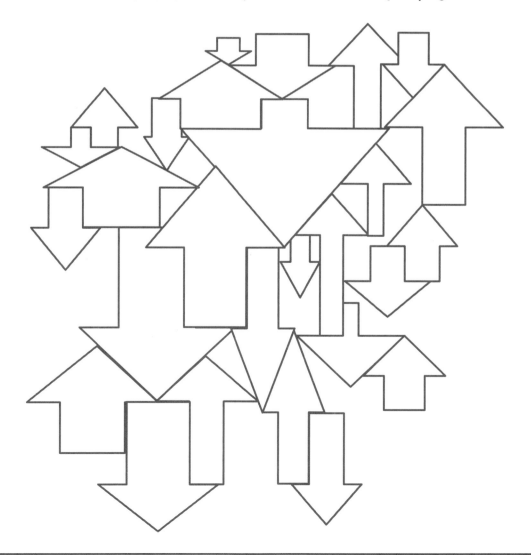

132. AFTER-WORDS

Which word can go after all these words to make new words?

B O O K _____

G O L F _____

Y O U T H _____

133. TOP TEN

Complete the word by filling the spaces with a whole number between one and ten.

O P P _ _ _ _ N T

134. CAMOUFLAGE

The name of a wild animal is hidden in the sentence below. Find it by joining words or parts of words together.

Well, I only asked a question!

135. ADDER

Using other words with the same meaning, can you create a new word from two separate ones?

YOUNG DOG — — —
+ **DOMESTIC ANIMAL** + — — —
────────────────────
= **MARIONETTE** =
— — — — — —

136. SNEAKY SNAKE

Which snake is the longest?

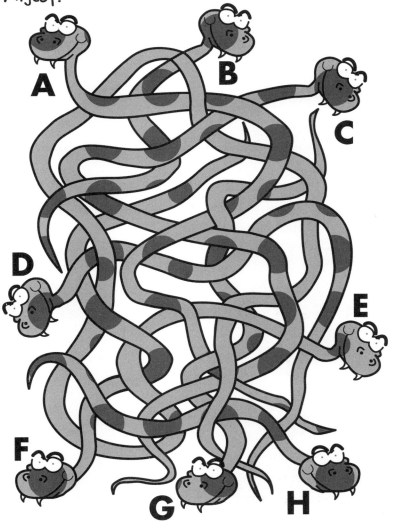

137. FACE FACTS

Use the letters that make up the face to make a name.

_ _ _ _ _

138. SPLITZER

This row of ten letters can be split into two five-letter words which relate to school. Words read from left to right and the letters are in the correct order. What are they?

C P L U A P S I L S

/
_____

139. MIND THE GAP

Which single three-letter word completes all of the following words?

_ _ _ _ C I L

O _ _ _ _

D E _ _ _ D

_ _ _ _ T A G O N

140. NUMBER-RING

Move around the circle. You have to write a number in the blank section that will continue the number pattern.

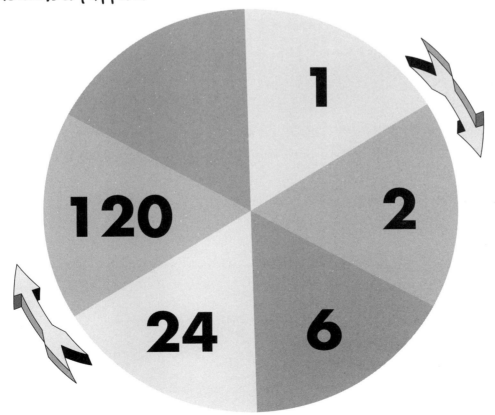

141. BACK WORDS

Solve the clues: the second answer is the first answer written backwards.

LOOK QUICKLY AND SECRETLY * **CONTINUE TO HAVE SOMETHING**

_ _ _ _ _ _   *   _ _ _ _ _ _

142. LINKS

Which word will go after the first word and before the second word?

L A W N (_ _ _ _ _ _) R A C K E T

143. ADDER

Using other words with the same meaning, can you create a new word from two separate ones?

BILL   _ _ _ _

+ PERMIT   **+** _ _ _ _

= PILL   **=**

_ _ _ _

144. RED CARNATION!

In the country of Redrov all vehicles are painted red. (That's why it's a red car nation!).

○ In the main street there are two red cars in front of a red car.

○ There are two red cars behind a red car.

○ The car in the middle of the line of traffic is red.

What's the least number of cars in the main street?

LEVEL ONE ANSWERS

1. CUBED
2

2. CLOTHES LINE
Jeans/Shirt.

3. JIGSAW
Danny went first and put in the piece bottom left. Tessa went second and put in the piece top left. Tim went third and put in the piece bottom right. Rosie went last and put in the piece top right.

4. AFTER-WORDS
out.

5. CREATURE CODE
Leopard.

6. CONNECTIONS

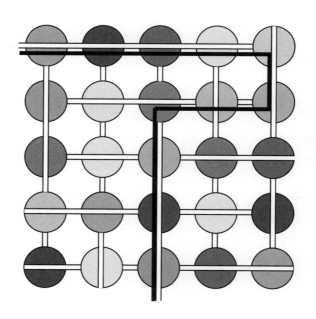

7. SECRET SEVEN

Pleased.

8. TOP TEN

one. This completes the word throne.

9. RUINED TEMPLE

Message reads: You are lost. Look at the page on its side. The writing is mirrored as well.

10. LINKS

Basket.

11. BACK WORDS

Spin * Nips.

12. ADDER

out + cry = outcry.

13. ACT 3

14. FRUIT SPLIT

orange is split between the words
HERO RAN GENEROUSLY.

15. SPIKE LIKES . . .

Spike likes things that sound like letters of the alphabet. Ps, Is and Us.

16. FACE FACTS

George.

17. CRAZY CREATURES

1. Mare
2. Stoat
3. Goat
4. Deer
5. Leopard.

18. GOING BATS

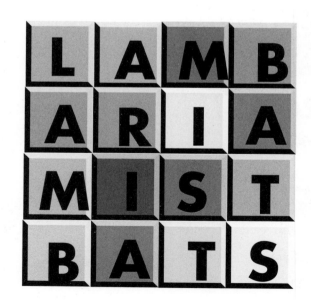

19. FLY THE FLAG
Paris.

20. SILHOUETTE
C.

21. MIND THE GAP
Rot.

22. COUNTER
12.

23. SECRET SEVEN
Peanuts.

24. CAR CHASE
Caravan.

25. WHAT'S NEXT?
U. Letters are in alphabetical order, with three missed out at each move.

26. AFTER-WORDS
Back.

27. STARGAZER
1. Tall
2. Troy
3. Part
4. Trap
5. Ploy
6. Tool.

28. NUMBER FIT

```
5   5   9   6       7 5 2 3 6 0
4 9 8   1 0 6 0   3   4   3
6   5   4   0   1 0 3 9 3 6 2
8 0 2 6 5   5         3
2   5       7 6 4 5   7 0 3 0
8 5 4   2 0 1 6   8       0
  4 1 8     7   9 3 9 4 0 6
  9   7 4 8 6 5 1 2       0
4 7 4 9 3 4   9     2 6 9
  6     0   8 1 0 7   9 2 2
9 8 4 4   6 0 8 2       6   0
    5       2   1 8 3 4 1
8 5 5 7 8 1 6   2   1   2   4
  7   8   4   9 5 4 3   3 1 9
8 1 4 0 7 3     9     9   7   5
```

29. ON LINE

Paste.

30. SECRET PLACES

1. Spain

2. Chile

3. Canada.

31. PATTERN PLAY

32. BACK WORDS

Stun * Nuts.

33. SPLITZER

Brass/Steel.

34. MIDDLE MOVES

1. Oil/Owl
2. Jig/Jog
3. Hip/Hop
4. Shirt/Short
5. Leaning/Leaping.

35. MORE OR LESS?

On average there are 30 days in a month, so 6 x 30 gives 180 – more than the number of hours in a week, which is 168.

36. JUST JUICE

100. Coming back you looked at the same cartons again.

37. WHAT AM I?
World.

38. NEWS ROUND
1. News
2. Nets
3. Pets
4. Peas
5. Peal
6. Seal
7. Seas
8. Sews.

39. ALPHA-SEARCH
Peach.

40. NUMBER RING
2. Each number is halved.

41. SALT SIGNS
1. Salt
2. Plate
3. Pepper.

42. LINKS
Pole.

43. BACK WORDS
Pets * Step.

44. CORNERED

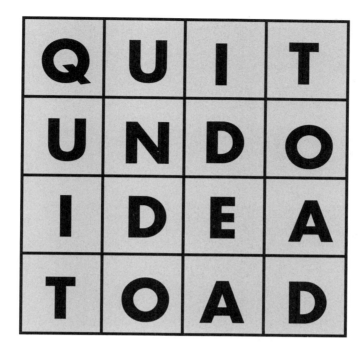

45. FACE FACTS

Carol.

46. ADDER

Not + Ice = Notice.

47. SHAPE UP!

1. Cone
2. Cube
3. Square
4. Circle
5. Triangle.

48. SECRET SEVEN

Potters.

49. STARTING BLOCKS
16.

50. AFTER-WORDS
over.

51. MIND THE GAP
And.

52. CALL ME A CAB!

```
          I T E M
          I T A X I
          E X I T     T
P L U M I T E D E N       N
L O S E       D O N E     E
U S E S       E N D S     S
M E S S O O N E S T
      O B O E
      O O Z E
      N E E D
```

53. SECRET SEVEN

Parsley.

54. NICE ICE

1. Ben/chocolate
2. Liza/orange
3. Alan/Vanilla
4. Katie/Pistachio.

55. IN THE BAG

You give your fifth friend the carrier bag with a baseball hat in it.

56. ADDER

War + Saw = Warsaw.

57. FIGURE FACES

C, which totals 22.

58. LINKS

Chop.

59. SPLIT UP

1 e,
2 c,
3 d,
4 f,
5 a,
6 b.

60. SECRET SEVEN

Parties.

61. TOP TEN

Two. This completes the word footwork.

62. DUNGEON DOOM

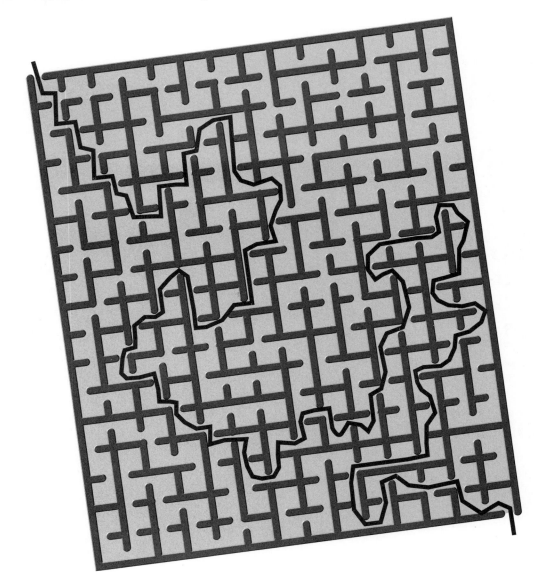

63. AFTER-WORDS

Stick.

64. YOUR DEAL

65. ADDER

Pal + Ace = Palace.

66. MIND THE GAP

Den.

67. BOXED IN

The cross features in six rectangles, and the star only features in five.

68. CAMOUFLAGE

Panther.

69. LINKS

Book.

70. NAME GAME

Jennifer.

71. SPLITZER

Boxer/corgi.

72. SHEEPISH

Number 6. Look at the EYES.

73. BACK WORDS

Edam * Made.

74. FRUITY

orange (use the letters in the words one rag).

75. METAL DETECTORS

1. Silver
2. Gold
3. Lead
4. Iron
5. Tin.

76. WHAT'S NEXT?

30. They are the number of days in calendar months starting with January.

77. TOP TEN

Nine. This completes the word canine.

78. PYRAMID

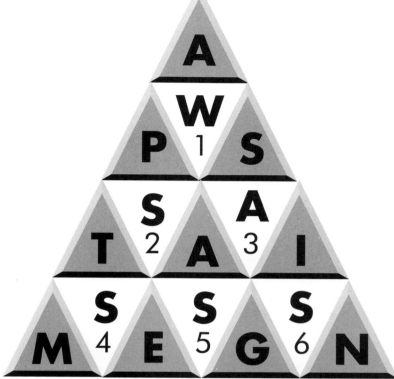

79. SECRET SEVEN
Parents.

80. CDS
32. The pop, dance and rock CDs make up seven eighths of the collection. That's half + a quarter + an eighth. The movie CDs must make up the remaining eighth. There are four of them. 8 x 4 = 32.

81. LINKS
Fall.

82. HAT TRICK

83. AFTER-WORDS

Drum.

84. SQUARE SEARCH

S	C	A	R	E
C	O	C	O	A
A	C	T	O	R
R	O	O	S	T
E	A	R	T	H

85. FRUIT CODE

1. Apple
2. Grape
3. Lemon
4. Cherry.

86. NOW YOU SEE IT...

7.

87. 'EAR' EAR

Three.

88. NUMBER-RING

15.

7 is taken away each time.

89. FACE FACTS

Dorothy.

90. SPLITZER

Beige/Green.

91. VIDEO PLUS

92. BACK WORDS

Gulp * Plug

93. CLOCK OUT

No 3. The minute hand moves back five minutes and the hour hand moves forward two hours with each move.

94. SECRET SEVEN

Plaster.

95. LINE UP

Both lines are the same length.

96. MIND THE GAP

End.

97. ADDER

Pea + Led = Pealed.

98. WINNING TICKET

A is Tony who won chocolates with ticket 555.
B is Laura who won the book with ticket 444.
C is Sarah who won the robot with ticket 246.
D is Steve who won the beachball with ticket 463.

99. AFTER-WORDS

Egg.

100. ON TARGET

18 + 39 + 43.

101. MOSAIC

102. SPLITZER
cocoa/water.

103. STACK SYSTEM
1. Artist
2. Start
3. Star
4. Rat
5. Tear
6. Earth
7. Father.

104. LINKS
Garden.

105. DIFFERENT DIGITS

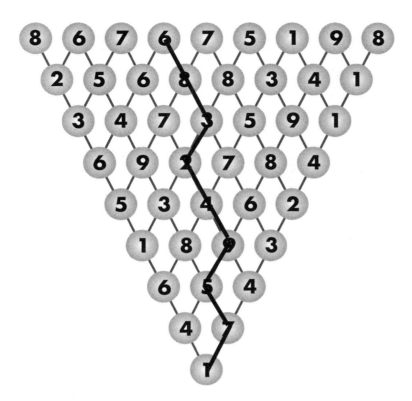

106. SECRET SEVEN

Notices.

107. CATNAP

1. Basket
2. Hutch
3. Kennel
4. Stable
5. Barn.

108. BACK WORDS

Swot * Tows.

109. MIND THE GAP

Card.

110. ADDER

Pan + Try = Pantry.

111. NUMBER-RING

78. 13 is added each time.

112. AWAY DAY

NOON. It reads the same forwards, backwards and when viewed upside down.

113. WHEELIES

Track nº 9.

114. FRUIT SPLIT

Apple is split between the words CLAP PLEASE.

115. TAKE SIDES

The pentagon. 14 pentagons have 70 sides. 23 triangles have 69 sides. 8 octagons have 64 sides.

116. LINKS

Kennel.

117. AFTER-WORDS

Band.

118. STARTING BLOCKS

119. SUM SHAPE

The green triangle is worth 5. Red circle is 1. 5 + 5 + 5 = 15.

120. MUSIC BOX

Harmonica.

121. S.O.S.

1. Sobs
2. Shouts
3. Spotless
4. Supporters
5. Scissors
6. Shorts
7. Sons.

122. WHAT'S NEXT?

P. Letters go backwards through the alphabet, with one missed out at each move.

123. CROSS PURPOSES

Piece D is not used.

124. RHYMER

Mouse.

125. MORE OR LESS?

The small hand of a clock goes on to 5 twice a day, making 14 times in a week. There are 13 letters in half of the alphabet.

126. MIND THE GAP

Ran.

127. BACK WORDS

Loot * Tool.

128. TWINS

2 and 6.

129. COMPU COMMAND

Print.

130. SECRET SEVEN

Scented.

131. POINTED

13 arrows point up, and 14 point down.

132. AFTER-WORDS

club.

133. TOP TEN

one. This completes the word opponent.

134. CAMOUFLAGE

Lion.

135. ADDER

Pup + Pet = Puppet.

136. SNEAKY SNAKE

Snake E.

137. FACE FACTS

Scott.

138. SPLITZER

Class/Pupil.

139. MIND THE GAP

Pen.

140. NUMBER-RING

720. First number is multiplied by 2, the second by 3, then by 4 and 5. 6 x 120 = 720.

141. BACK WORDS

Peek * Keep.

142. LINKS

Tennis.

143. ADDER

Tab + Let = Tablet.

144. RED CARNATION!

Three cars.

LEVEL TWO QUESTIONS

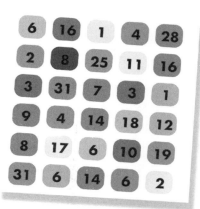

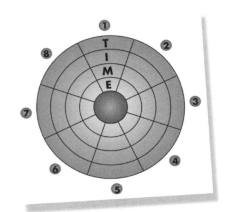

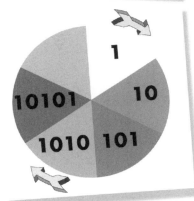

I. BEAM ME UP

In a computer game you have captured three different warriors - an X-fighter, a Yarg and a Zeneck.

○ You have to move all three of them from zone A to zone B. The only way to do this is by transporter beam. No more than two people can be in the beam at any one time, and you must be travelling every time the transporter beam is used.

○ The X-fighter has declared he will attack the Yarg if he gets the chance.

○ The Yarg has declared he will attack the Zeneck if he gets the chance.

○ The Zeneck has agreed that he will not be involved in any more fighting.

○ How many journeys will you have to make between zone A and zone B to make sure that the troublesome trio are all safely transported to zone B?

X-FIGHTER   YARG   ZENECK

ZONE A   ZONE B

X+ Y+ Z+ YOU

2. MIND THE GAP

Which single three-letter word completes all of the following words?

K I _ _ _ R A M

C O _ _ _ N E

S _ _ _ A N

A P O _ _ _ I S E

3. AFTER WORDS

Which word can go after all these words to make new words?

H A L F _____

L I F E _____

S O M E _____

4. FOLDED

Which of these cubes would be made if the shape shown in the centre was folded?

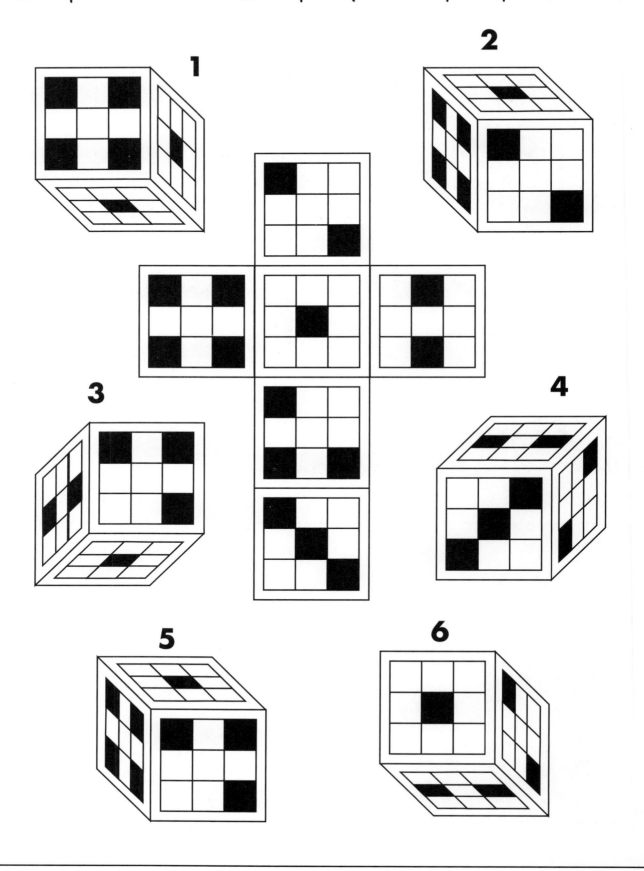

5. RED ALERT

Top security! Secret message! Move each letter to its linked empty circle to read the message.

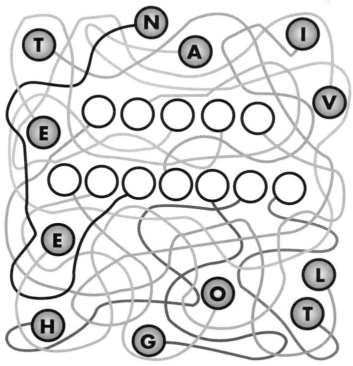

6. INSTRUMENTAL

Shapes and signs have been used to take the place of letters of the alphabet. Can you work out what the words are? They are all musical instruments.

❄	✧	😐	💣	🚩	👉	❄
T	R	U	M	P	E	T

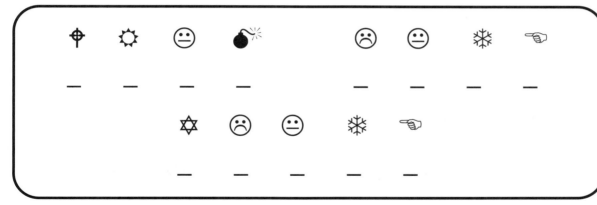

✟	✧	😐	💣		☹	😐	❄	👉
_	_	_	_		_	_	_	_

✡	☹	😐	❄	👉
_	_	_	_	_

7. STRAIGHT AND CROOKED

Here are four triangles and two squares. There are 20 straight lines used to form these shapes. Can you make four triangles and two squares by using just eight straight lines?

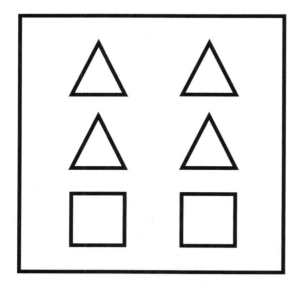

CLUE

You cannot do this by thinking about the shapes being on their own!

Better clue:
We've never said the shapes have to be the same size as those shown here!

Even Better Clue:
Think of a square within a square!

8. SAD START

With the word SAD in place, can you fit all these words containing three letters back into the frame?

ANT	OIL
ASP	OWN
AXE	SAD
DIP	SIP
EMU	SIX
EWE	SPA
FEE	TEE
FLY	TOE
GNU	USE
GOT	YOU

9. SPLITZER

This row of ten letters can be split into two five-letter words which are the names of two joints in the body. Words read from left to right and the letters are in the correct order. What are they?

E A L N B K O L E W

/

_____

10. TIME OUT

The name of a period of time is hidden in each of the sentences below. Find the names by joining words or parts of words together. The first is done for you.

We shall finis**H OUR** meal and then go out.

They start to play earlier in summer.

He produced a yellow umbrella.

I hope it will be calm on the sea.

11. SPINNER

Rearrange each horizontal word to make a new five-letter word. When the grid is complete the shaded vertical column will spell out another word.

S	W	E	A	T
M	A	P	L	E
H	O	R	S	E
S	W	O	R	D
S	T	O	V	E

12. FIFTH DIMENSION

Start on the top line and move from number to number, going down or sideways, to reach the bottom line. You can only land on numbers which can be divided exactly by 5.

15	8	10	6	37	17
12	30	25	36	40	50
70	65	13	8	16	12
21	70	25	35	50	40
50	40	32	60	46	30
17	24	50	16	28	60

13. ADDER

Using other words with the same meaning, can you create a new word from two separate ones?

ARMED CONFLICT   _ _ _

+ LION'S HOME   _ _ _

= BIG GAME PROTECTOR   _ _ _ _ _ _

14. SPACE TREK

Which of the space portals logs on to a flight path that leads to a safe landing?

15. SECRET SEVEN

Rearrange the letters in the word below to make another word of seven letters.

T	E	D	I	O	U	S
_	_	_	_	_	_	_

CLUE

Think
NOT INDOORS

16. TAKE OFF

Which plane is the next to take off? Use the clues to identify it.

The nose is rounded.
The tail is dark.
The wings have stripes on them.
There's a circle on the side.

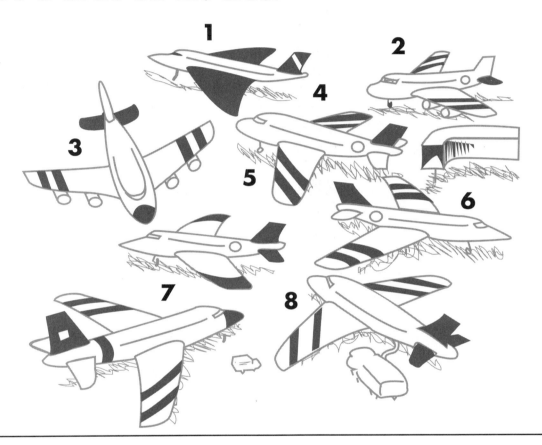

17. BACK WORDS

Solve the clues: the second answer is the first answer written backwards.

THEY SUPPORT THE TEETH * SELF SATISFIED

_ _ _ _ _ * _ _ _ _ _

18. STACK SYSTEM

As you work down the stack, remove a letter from your answer to get the next answer.

once you've reached answer four, you then add a letter each time until you reach the bottom of the stack. You can change the order of the letters if you need to.

1 Small church *(6 letters)*

2 Not expensive *(5 letters)*

3 Coat without sleeves *(4 letters)*

4 Hat *(3 letters)*

5 Applaud *(4 letters)*

6 Location *(5 letters)*

7 Royal house *(6 letters)*

19. LINKS

which word will go after the first word and before the second word?

T A B L E (_ _ _ _ _ _) R A C K E T

20. VANISHING POINT

In this puzzle you have to search out the things that aren't there! Here's a jumble of letters of the alphabet. Each letter appears once, except for some letters which do not appear at all. First, work out the missing letters then arrange them to spell out the name of something you don't want to see!

You need to discover five letters.

21. TRIANGLE TEST

How many triangles are there in this pattern?

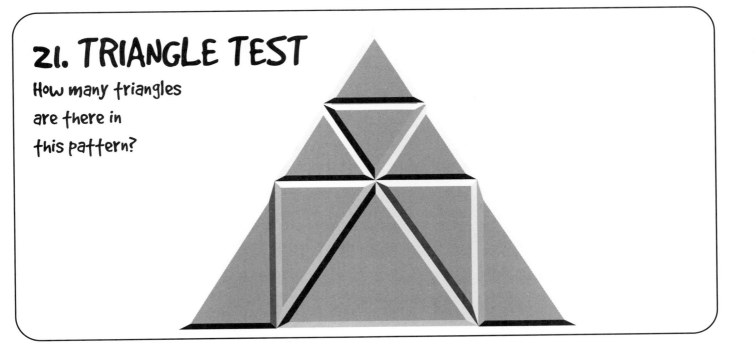

22. BACK NUMBERS

Put the numbers back so that each line of three numbers adds up to the same number.

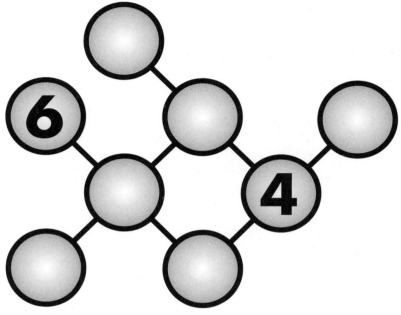

2	3	4	5	6	7	8	9

23. MORE OR LESS?

Which is greater – the number of days in seven weeks, or the number of spaces between the spokes of a two wheel bicycle that has 24 spokes on each wheel?

Monday
Tuesday
Wednesday
Thursday
Friday
Saturday
Sunday

24. COMPUTER CODE

Shapes and signs have been used to take the place of letters of the alphabet. The first group of symbols stands for the word COMPUTER. What computer-linked word does the second group make?

C O M P U T E R

_ _ _ _ _ _ _

25. MIND THE GAP

Which single three-letter word completes all of the following words?

N I _ _ _ E E N

B R U _ _ _ T E

M A G _ _ _ I Z E

P L A _ _ _ S

26. SEEING DOUBLE

There are two crossword grids and two clues for each space. Which answer fits which grid? That's for you to decide! There's a one-word start.

ACROSS

1 Spinning toy * Rubbish pile (3) 5 Not on time * Command to stay still (4)

6 Moisture on the ground at daybreak * Garden peas grow inside this (3)

8 On no occasion * Human - looking moving machine (5)

11 Move quickly * Quarrel (3) 12 Orange skin * Applaud (4)

13 Jewel * Male sheep (3)

DOWN

2 Metal * Above (4) 3 Guide or drive * Used for shaving (5)

4 Fast plane * Secret agent (3) 7 Hold up * Grown-up girls (5)

9 Thick string * Type of fish you can eat (4)

10 Monkey * Frozen water (3)

27. SQUARE SEARCH

A word square reads the same whether looked at going across or down. You need to find five words in the letter grid that can be used to form a word square. The first word has been found for you.

S	P	A	R	E
P				
A				
R				
E				

28. WHAT'S NEXT?

What is the next letter to go in the space?

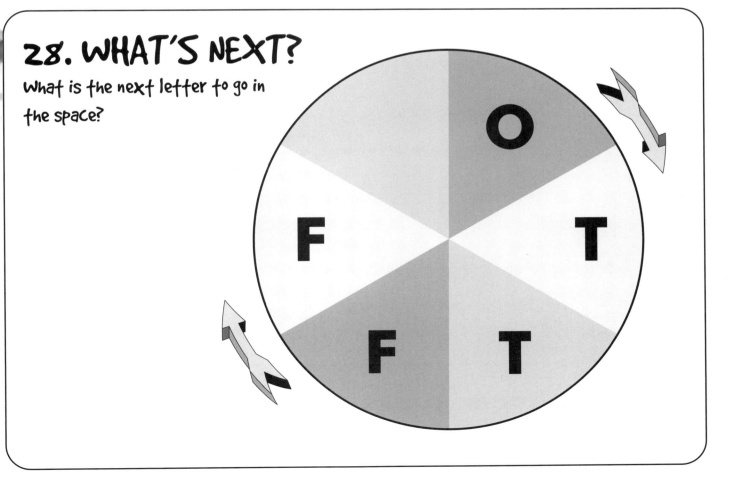

29. PYRAMID

Fit all the words back into the pyramid grid. Each word is written in a mini-pyramid shape. The first letter of each word goes in a numbered space. The second letter goes in the space directly above, the third letter goes to the right and the fourth letter goes to the left. There's a one-letter start, but – be warned – there's only one solution!

ALSO
APEX
AXLE
FELL
SEWN
SLOW

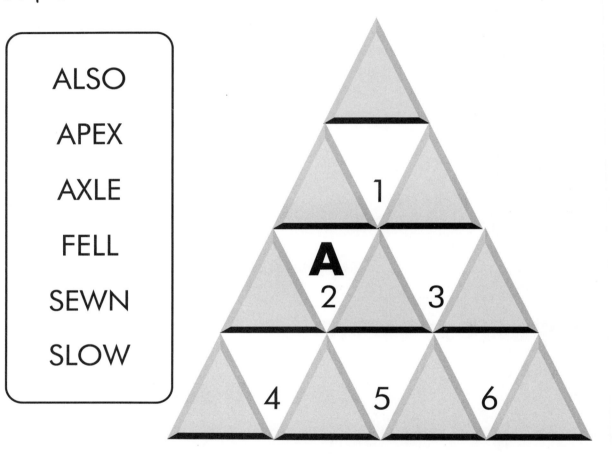

30. FRUIT SPLIT

The name of a fruit is hidden in the sentence below. Find it by joining words or parts of words together.

He felt anger in everyone's expressions.

31. TOP TEN

Complete the word by filling the spaces with a whole number between ONE and TEN.

1

6

4

LIS _ _ _ _ ED

2 5

32. TAKING SHAPE

Which pair of shapes appear on a linked pathway?

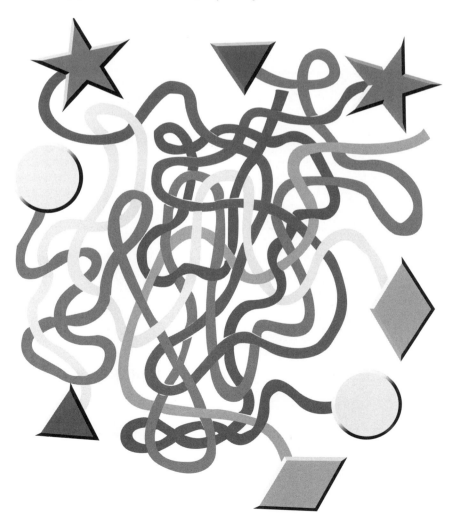

33. MIDDLE MOVES

Each clue has two answers. The two answer words are spelled the same except that the middle letters are different.

Evergreen tree with cones ✱ In favour of *(3 letters)*
ANSWERS: _____

Plan of the Earth or roads ✱ Use this to clean a floor
(3 letters)
ANSWERS: _____

Structure over an oil well ✱ Mat *(3 letters)*
ANSWERS: _____

Third month ✱ Sports fixture *(5 letters)*
ANSWERS: _____

Going in front ✱ Departing *(7 letters)*
ANSWERS: _____

34. SECRET SEVEN

Rearrange the letters in the word below to make another word of seven letters.

G A T E M A N

_ _ _ _ _ _ _

CLUE

Think PINK

35. CLOG-WORK!

You'll have your work cut out to find a pair of identical Dutch clogs. Which two are identical?

1

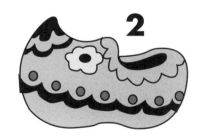
2

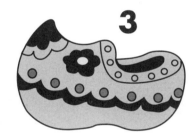
3

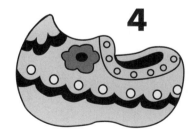
4

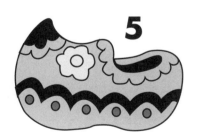
5

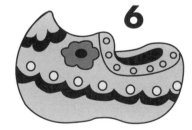
6

7

8

9

36. STRANGE SIGNS

Which of the strange signs should go in the empty space to continue the pattern?

?

A

B

C

D

37. FACE FACTS

Use the letters that make up the face to make a name.

38. ADDER

Using other words with the same meaning, can you create a
new word from two separate ones?

HUMOUR ___ ___ ___

+ OPPOSITE OF HIM ___ ___ ___

= SHRIVEL

___ ___ ___ ___ ___ ___

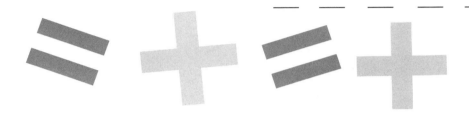

39. AFTER-WORDS

Which word can go after all these words to make new words?

F I S H _____

P A N _____

R O C K _____

40. LINKS

Which word will go after the first word and before the second word?

F R E S H (_ _ _) H O S T E S S

41. NUMBER FIT

Fit all the numbers back into the frame.

3 DIGITS

140	327	519	657	874
242	438	565	782	936

4 DIGITS

1023	3042	5264	7350	8403	9638
2033	3953	6239	7707	8832	
2092	5202	6789	8383	9016	

5 DIGITS

29525   42928   76381   98142

6 DIGITS

137762	295459	462093	709342
240808	378915	584631	821287

7 DIGITS

1013974	4281499	7205357
3757122	5839243	9677065

42. SPLITZER

This row of ten letters can be split into two five-letter words which are the names of two parts of a car. Words read from left to right and the letters are in the correct order. What are they?

B R W A H E E K L E

/
_____

43. BURIED TREASURE

Captain Skint and his pirate crew are burying their treasure.

Five pirates dig five holes in five hours.

All the pirates dig at the same speed, and all the holes in the ground are the same size.

How long would it take one pirate to dig one hole to hide the treasure?

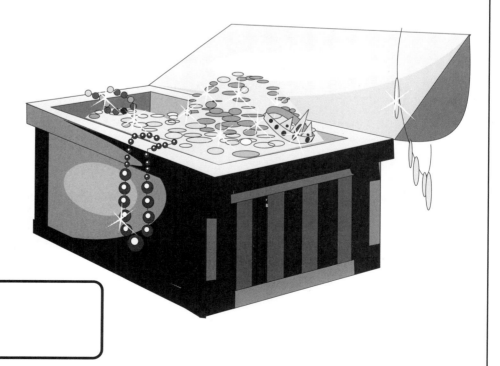

44. BACK WORDS

Solve the clues: the second answer is the first answer written backwards.

PUT AN END TO * **PANS**

_ _ _ _   *   _ _ _ _

45. FEEDING TIME

Use the words below to make two word squares. Each square must contain the word EATS.

AREA   **EATS**   **REAL**   **TEAM**

EATS   **ELSE**   **SAME**   **TREE**

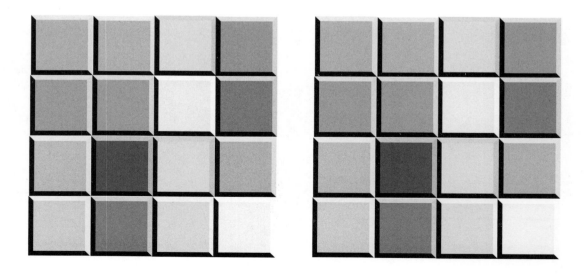

46. NUMBER-RING

Move around the circle. You have to write a number in the blank section that will continue the number pattern.

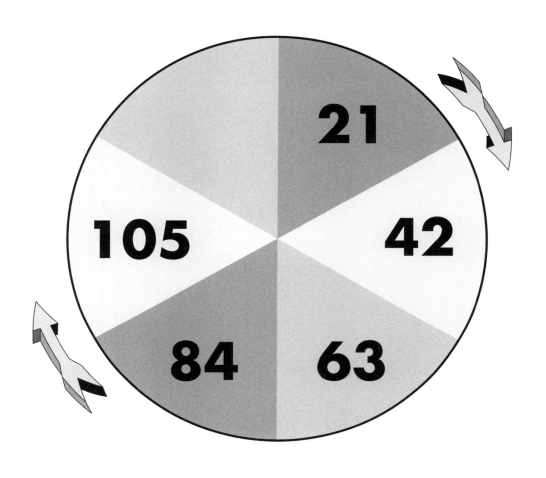

47. SECRET SEVEN

Rearrange the letters in the word below to make another word of seven letters.

S	E	M	I	N	A	R
_	_	_	_	_	_	_

CLUE

Think
NAVAL FORCE

48. WHAT AM I?

My first is in chair
But isn't in chain.

My second's in pale
And also in pain.

My third is in edge
But isn't in green.

My fourth is in lime
But isn't in mean.

My fifth's in cone,
And also in round.

Do you know what I am?
I'm connected with sound!

49. MIND THE GAP

Which single four-letter word completes all of the following words?

_ _ _ _ M U N K

_ _ _ _ B O A R D

M I C R O _ _ _ _

50. STARGAZER

All answers contain four letters and follow the direction shown by the arrows.

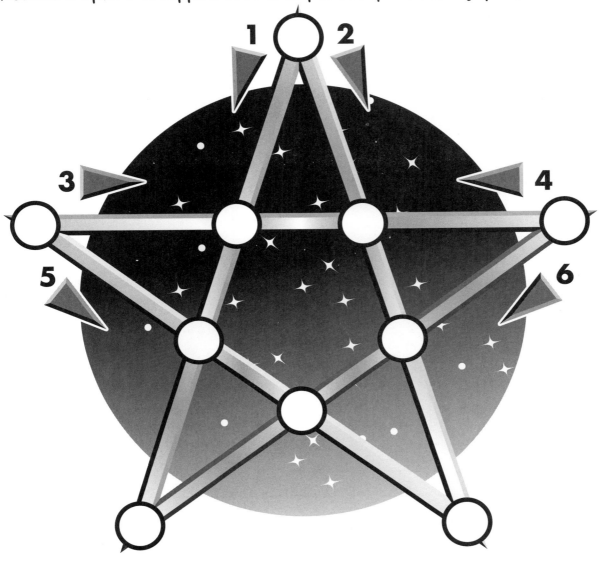

1. Scottish tartan skirt
2. Tied rope
3. Pointed items that go with needles
4. Cut carefully with scissors
5. Scheme
6. Black deposit found in a chimney

51. MOSAIC

Fit the letter tiles back into the frame. When the tiles fit together in the right order, the mosaic has five words reading across, and four words reading down.

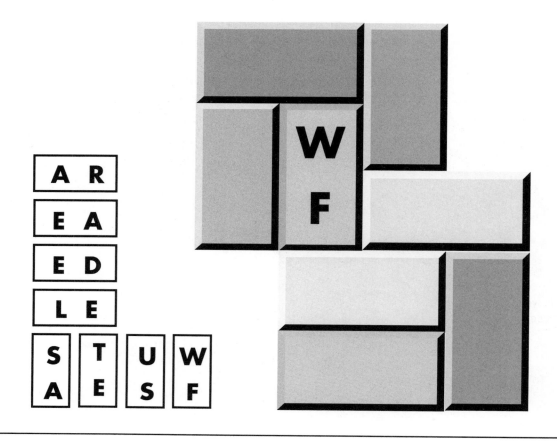

52. COLLECTORS

Dan collects odd numbers and Fran collects even numbers.

One of Dan's numbers is subtracted from one of Fran's numbers.

Who will collect the number that is the answer to the subtraction?

53. BROTHERS AND SISTERS

Here are four pairs of brothers and sisters. From the comments made, can you name each person and pair them together?

My sister Sally has blonde hair.

Rebecca isn't my sister.

Julie's my sister.

Richard and Mark have sisters with blonde hair.

My brother Paul is wearing a baseball hat.

Paul and Mark are the boys wearing glasses. Neither is my brother.

My brother is called David.

I'm not Alice.

54. TAKE SIDES

Look at the shapes below and work out which group has most sides.

x 20   x 27   x 16

55. ADDER

Using other words with the same meaning, can you create a new word from two separate ones?

NOT ON   __ __ __ __

+ FINISH   __ __ __

= INSULT   __ __ __ __ __ __ __

56. LOST LANDS

The name of a country is hidden in each of the sentences below. Find them by joining words or parts of words together.

> He went to teach in a school close by.

> He broke the tape running at speed.

> The staff ran certainly as fast as the pupils.

57. RING OF FIRE

Solve each clue and write the answers into the spaces in the grid. All answers have four letters. Put the first letter in the outer circle, then move towards the centre. Only one letter changes between answers, and answer 8 will be only one letter different from answer 1.

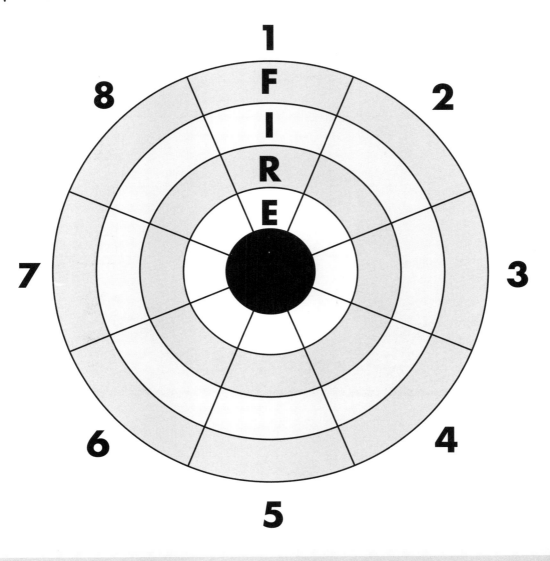

(1) Burning wood
(2) Use this to smooth fingernails
(3) Add liquid to the top
(4) Tumble over
(5) Very high
(6) Cash register in a store
(7) Glazed piece for a mosaic
(8) Show signs of getting weary

58. REPEATER

Solve the clues and fit the words into the grid. The last three letters of one word are the first three of the next.

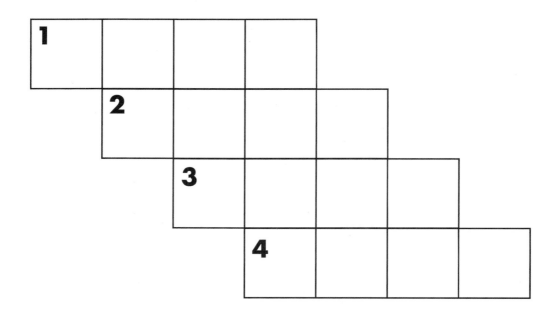

1 Mark left by a wound   **2** Look after
3 Region   **4** Not fake

59. ON LINE

Add one line to complete each letter and spell out a computer-linked command.

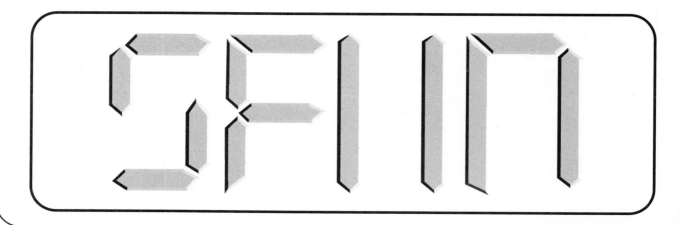

60. TEN TIMES

Try to find this number ten times in the grid.

972553

9	3	9	5	7	9	7	3	9	7	2	5
3	7	9	7	2	3	5	9	2	7	9	7
2	9	2	3	9	5	9	7	2	5	5	3
7	9	3	5	2	3	7	2	9	2	7	9
9	7	3	7	5	9	3	5	7	5	7	7
7	2	9	3	9	3	7	5	3	2	9	2
3	5	2	3	2	8	2	3	5	9	7	5
9	5	9	7	7	2	7	5	9	7	3	5
7	3	5	2	3	9	3	2	3	2	7	3
2	9	7	2	5	5	3	5	7	5	2	9
7	2	7	3	7	9	7	3	9	5	7	2
2	9	5	7	5	9	7	5	2	3	2	9

61. BACK WORDS

Solve the clues: the second answer is the first answer written backwards.

RUN LIKE A RIVER * **ANIMAL WHICH HUNTS IN PACKS**

_ _ _ _ * _ _ _ _

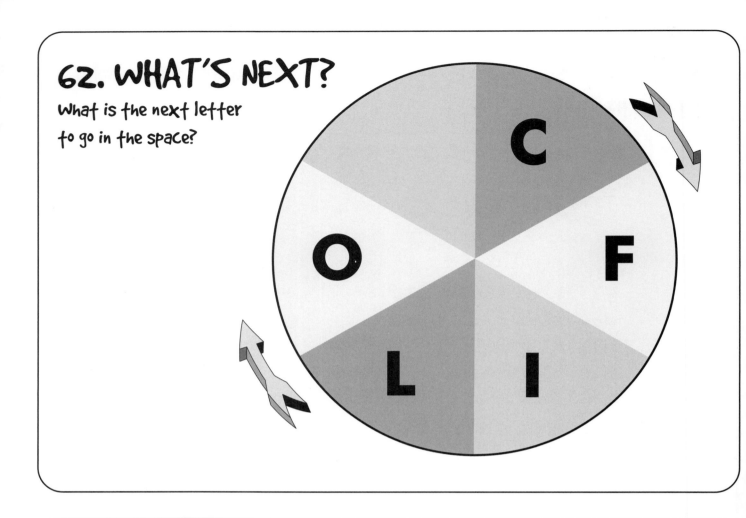

62. WHAT'S NEXT?

What is the next letter to go in the space?

C

F

O

I

L

63. ANIMAL TRACKS

Make tracks and find seven different animals in the grid. Start at the letter in the top left square and move in any direction except diagonally. Every letter is used once.

C	A	M	E	A	R
L	L	E	B	L	E
I	A	R	D	E	P
O	P	E	G	I	H
N	O	R	E	T	A
L	E	A	P	T	N

64. THE LAST STRAW

Which glass does the straw go into?

65. SECRET SEVEN

Rearrange the letters in the word below to make another word of seven letters.

T H I C K E N

_ _ _ _ _ _ _

CLUE

Think
COOKERY ROOM

66. BOWLING

Four friends go ten-pin bowling together.

They decide that they will each play each other once.

How many games will they play?

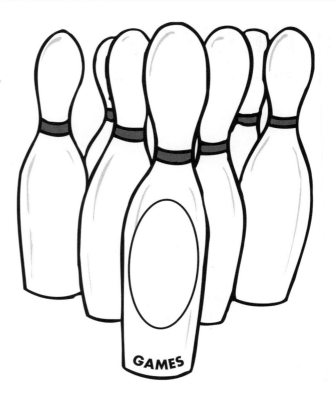

67. STORMY WEATHER!

Use the groups of letters to name different types of nasty weather!

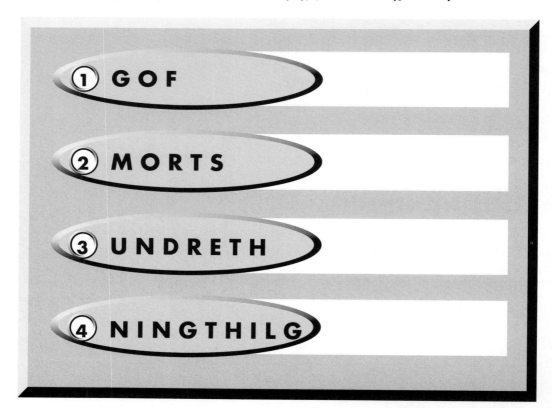

(1) G O F

(2) M O R T S

(3) U N D R E T H

(4) N I N G T H I L G

68. TIME TOTAL

What is more, the number of hours in four days or the months in eight years?

69. ODD ONE OUT

Which word is the odd one out, and why?

TRACE   **CATER**   **ACTOR**   **REACT**

70. SHOW TIME

Two mothers and two daughters bought tickets for the theatre.

The family sat together in the same row.

Each lady had a seat to herself.

Tickets cost ten pounds each. What is the least amount that the family could have paid?

71. AFTER WORDS
Which word can go after all these words to make new words?

L O N G _____

S T I L L _____

W I L D _____

72. MIND THE GAP
Which single three-letter word completes all of the following words?

T R O _ _ _ R S

A M _ _ _ D

H O _ _ _ S

M O _ _ _ T R A P

73. HALF TIME

The last two letters of one answer form the first half of the following answer.

1. As well as
2. Music performed by one person
3. Soft part of the ear
4. The most excellent
5. Wound with a knife
6. Competent, talented
7. Jump

1			
2			
3			
4			
5			
6			
7			

74. BREAKERS

This row of ten letters can be split into two five-letter words which are the names of two watery places. Words read from left to right and the letters are in the correct order.
What are they?

M	S	A	W	R	A	M	S	H	P

/

_____

75. DOMINOES

Put the dominoes back into the frame. Each row across, each column down and each diagonal from corner to corner must contain a black, white, grey and spotty square.

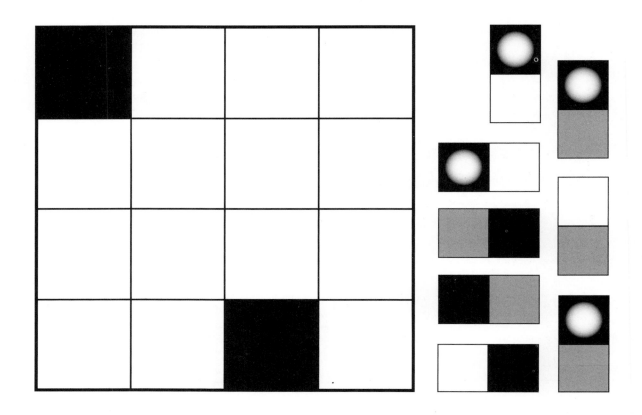

76. FACE FACTS

Use the letters that make up the face to make a name.

77. FAIR AND SQUARE

Four of the five listed words can be used to make a word square, which will read the same across and down. Which word is not needed?

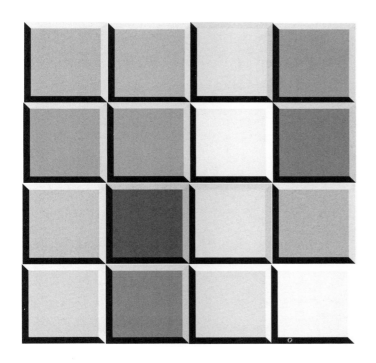

ELSE

EVER

REEL

VALE

VEIN

78. BODY LANGUAGE

Complete the words below by inserting the names of parts of the body.

S U N _ _ _ _ E

C H _ _ _ I N G

C _ _ _ _ _ M A N

79. WORKPLACE

Rearrange the letters in the words below to spell out names of different workers.

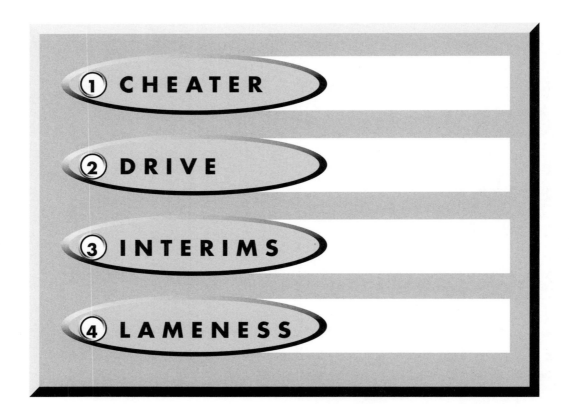

1. **CHEATER**
2. **DRIVE**
3. **INTERIMS**
4. **LAMENESS**

80. NUMBER-RING

Move around the circle.
You have to write a number
in the blank section that will
continue the number pattern.

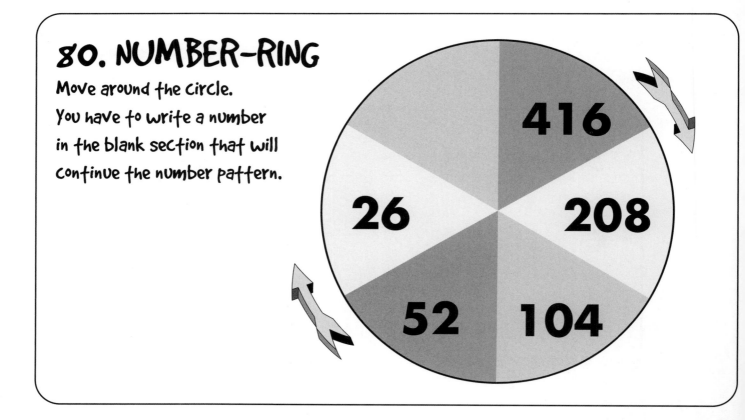

416

208

104

52

26

81. ADDER

Using other words with the same meaning, can you create a new word from two separate ones?

FIVE + FIVE   _ _ _

+ CRAWLING INSECT   _ _ _
_____

= PERSON WHO   _ _ _ _ _ _
  RENTS A FLAT

82. HOW MANY?

If A has three, B has one, C has none, D has one and E has four. How many will F have?

83. WHO'S THAT GIRL?

Rearrange the letters in the word below to make a girl's name of seven letters.

A I M L E S S

84. HAUNTED HOUSE

The haunted house is so spooky that even the names of the rooms are starting to vanish. Add one straight line to each shape to form letters that name the haunted rooms.

85. LINKS

Which word will go after the first word and before the second word?

CRAB (_ _ _ _ _) PIE

86. HALF CENTURY

Which line contains numbers that add up to exactly 50?

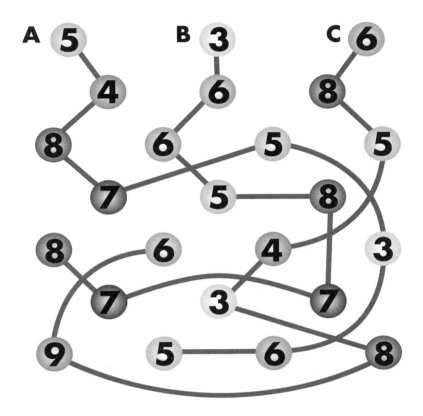

87. SPLITZER

This row of ten letters can be split into two five-letter words which are the names of two kitchen items. Words read from left to right and the letters are in the correct order.

What are they?

K S P N I O F O E N

/

88. SIGN PLEASE

Can you add two different mathematical signs into this line of numbers to make a sum that makes sense?

$$8 \quad 8 \quad 0 \quad 4 \quad 0 \quad 0 \quad 0 \quad 4 \quad 8 \quad 0$$

CLUE One of those signs is an equals sign

89. ON THE WILD SIDE

In this code, shapes and signs have been used to take the place of letters of the alphabet. The first group makes ELEPHANT.

Which creature is in code in the second group?

E L E P H A N T

90. TOP TEN

Complete the word by filling the spaces with a whole number between ONE and TEN.

1
6
4
D R I F _ _ _ _ O D
2
5

91. MIND THE GAP

Which single three-letter word completes all of the following words?

A N T I _ _ _ E

P O L K A _ _ _ S

_ _ _ _ T Y

A N E C _ _ _ E

92. LINKS

Which word will go after the first word and before the second word?

R I V E R (_ _ _ _) R O B B E R

93. BACK WORDS

Solve the clues: the second answer is the first answer written backwards.

HOLE IN THE GROUND * UPPER EDGE

___ ___ ___ ___ * ___ ___ ___ ___

94. LEAD ON!

Which lead belongs to the dog?

A B C D E F

95. SECRET SEVEN

Rearrange the letters in the word below to make another word of seven letters.

L A T C H E S

_ _ _ _ _ _ _

CLUE

Think
SWISS HOUSES

96. S FOR STARTERS

The first day of the month is a Saturday.

The month is not February.

How many days in the month will begin with a letter S?

97. AFTER WORDS

Which word can go after all these words to make new words?

B A C K _____

C A M P _____

W I L D _____

98. PASS NUMBER

Try and work out the pass number.

The number contains the five digits from 1 to 5.

The highest digit appears first.

The fifth digit is an even number.

The fourth digit minus the fifth gives the third.

INSERT
PASS NUMBER

99. FACE FACTS

Use the letters that make up the face to make a name.

100. ALPHABET

Move from circle to circle, beginning on the black circle and ending on the letter S. You have to move forward in alphabetical order.

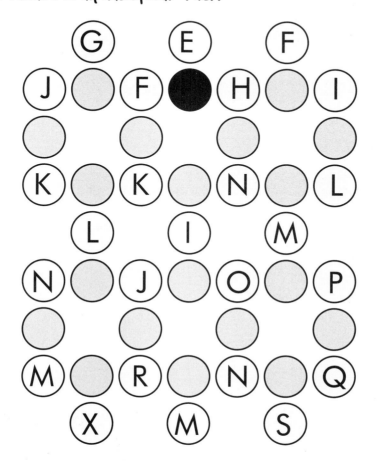

101. QUARTERBACK

A word square reads the same across and down. Fit the listed words back to make four word squares, each containing four words. One word is in position to start you off.

ACTS   PROP
ALTO   REAL
AREA   SOAP
CAST   STAG
LUMP   TALL
MEMO   TART
ONCE   TOGS
PEST   USER

102. SECRET SEVEN

Rearrange the letters in the word below to make another word of seven letters.

D O N A T O R

_ _ _ _ _ _ _

CLUE

Think
STRONG WIND

103. MIND THE GAP

Which single four-letter word completes all of the following words?

_ _ _ _ _ U R E

_ _ _ _ _ I L E S

C O N _ _ _ _

P R E _ _ _ _

104. I-SPY

There's a special sign that these spies give so they can be identified. Three of the spies shown here know what the secret sign is.

One person doesn't know what the sign is. Which one is it?

105. DIVIDERS

Start on the top line. Move from number to number, down or sideways to reach the bottom line. You can only land on numbers which can be divided exactly by 3.

9	32	7	8	12	9
3	2	9	9	13	3
15	9	3	18	19	9
7	6	21	5	24	4
6	13	27	18	3	6
9	8	20	16	13	12

106. AFTER-WORDS

Which word can go after all these words to make new words?

H O R N _____

H O S E _____

W I N D _____

107. FIRST CHANGE

Each clue has two answers. The two answer words are spelt the same except that the first letter of the second answer has changed in the alphabet.

So, for example, if answer one was BAT the second answer would be CAT.

1 Lion's lair ✳ 50 ÷ 5

ANSWERS: _____

2 Sleep on it! ✳ Scarlet

ANSWERS: _____

3 Silly ✳ Platform of floating logs

ANSWERS: _____

4 Present ✳ Pick up

ANSWERS: _____

5 Young hen ✳ Opposite of thin

ANSWERS: _____

108. HOW MANY?

How many circles can you count in the picture?

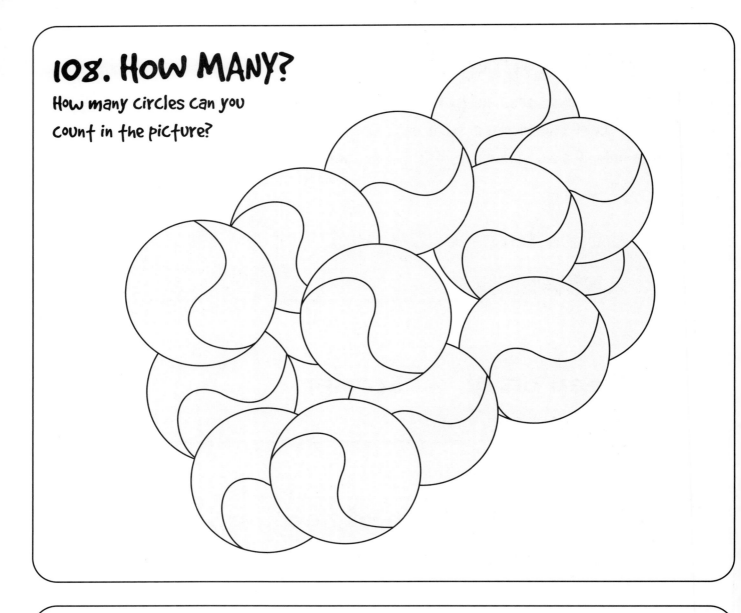

109. ADDER

Using other words with the same meaning, can you create a new word from two separate ones?

FRIEND ___ ___ ___ ___

+ PERMITTED ___ ___ ___

= STORAGE FRAME OR PLATFORM ___ ___ ___ ___ ___ ___ ___

110. NUMBER-RING

Move around the circle. You have to write a number in the blank section that will continue the number pattern.

111. SPLITZER

This row of ten letters can be split into two five-letter words which are the names of two colours. Words read from left to right and the letters are in the correct order. What are they?

BROWHOIWTNE

/
_____

112. ON GUARD

There are four robot guards patrolling this sector. They each look after an identically shaped area. Can you work out how the sector is divided?

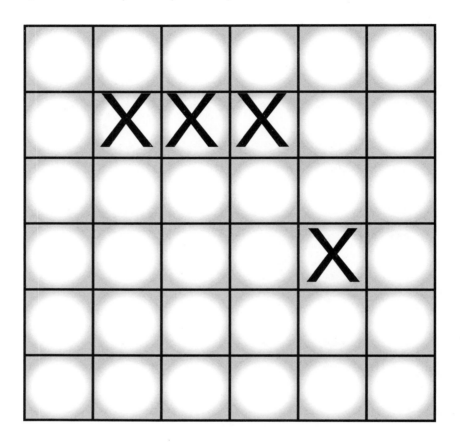

113. BACK WORDS

Solve the clues: the second answer is the first answer written backwards.

BE IN CHARGE OF A NEWSPAPER * **SEA MOVEMENT**

_ _ _ _ * _ _ _ _

114. WHAT'S NEXT?

What is the next letter to go in the space?

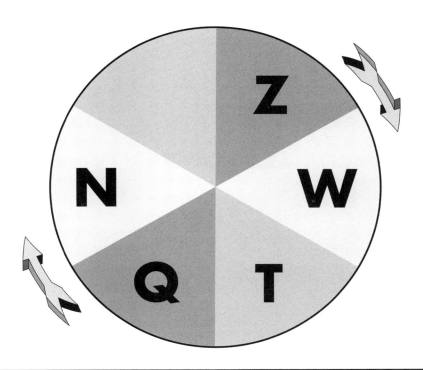

115. LIFT OFF

The groups of letters are arranged in alphabetical order. Move them round to spell out parts of an aeroplane.

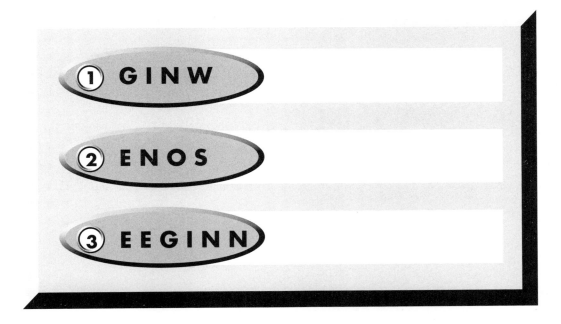

① GINW

② ENOS

③ EEGINN

116. NUMBER NAMES

In these names each of the different letters used have been given a numerical value. The total value of each word is reached by adding up the individual letter values.

I A N	6
A N N	8
T I N A	10
A N I T A	___

117. WHAT'S MISSING?

THR'S SOMTHING NDD TO COMPLT TH SNTNC.

118. RHYMER

My first is in mouse
But isn't in seat

My second's in boat
But isn't in beat.

My third is in bad
But isn't in bat.

My fourth is in them
But isn't in that.

My fifth is in much,
But isn't in check.

And just a small clue
There's a link with hi tech!

119. JUICY!

The name of a fruit juice is hidden in each of the sentences below. Find them by joining words or parts of words together.

1 Everything went wrong for Angela.

2 I haven't missed a single Monday at school.

3 Still, I'm expecting a good game.

120. LUCKY NUMBERS

Try your luck at searching out these numbers in the grid! The numbers always go in a straight line.

```
1 8 2 3 7 2 1 1 8 2 3 1
8 4 0 8 3 5 8 7 7 4 8 7
2 0 7 3 1 6 4 2 0 9 5 0
3 9 8 2 7 0 2 3 8 2 1 9
1 8 3 1 9 2 3 6 4 1 6 9
4 1 4 0 3 8 6 0 0 3 8 4
7 8 3 4 1 4 5 8 9 4 5 0
0 6 9 8 6 6 3 3 2 0 7 8
1 8 5 5 3 0 1 8 2 9 8 4
6 6 9 5 5 8 0 7 8 0 9 0
8 4 5 2 1 2 2 3 6 5 0 7
3 1 8 6 8 6 9 2 3 4 5 8
```

14729	31470	44600	59024	70563
17099	34956	49213	60474	72054
20731	37211	52122	63320	90361
25602	42365	53613	65516	92345

121. SECRET SEVEN

Rearrange the letters in the word below to make another word of seven letters.

E N L A R G E

_ _ _ _ _ _ _

CLUE

Think
ARMY OFFICER

122. LINE NINE

Answer each clue with a three letter word. Take the three answers in each group and use their nine letters to make the special Line Nine Word.

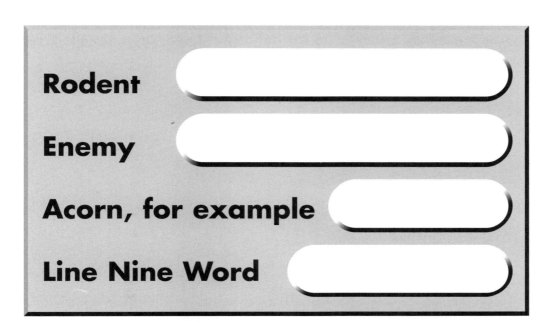

Rodent

Enemy

Acorn, for example

Line Nine Word

123. BALANCING ACT

Here's the amazing Balancing Twins performing their stage act. Which pole is the longer of the two?

124. MEAL DEAL

Four friends meet up for lunch. When they get the final bill they have the problem of dividing it. They have all ordered different things and shared them amongst themselves.

Donna comes up with a logical solution for sorting out the bill, even though it doesn't go in her favour! She puts in 4.

Carol thinks it's unfair but puts in 3. Alice's contribution is 1.

That leaves Beth. How much will she pay and why?

125. MIND THE GAP

Which single three-letter word completes all of the following words?

H A _ _ _ A T

O R _ _ _ E D

A M _ _ _ I O N

R A B _ _ _

126. CAMOUFLAGE

The name of a wild animal is hidden in the sentence below. Find it by joining words or parts of words together.

Apathy enables others to put their minority ideas into practice.

127. BATH TIME

In this code, letters have been replaced by symbols. The first group stands for SHAMPOO, and all the other words are items that are found in the bathroom.

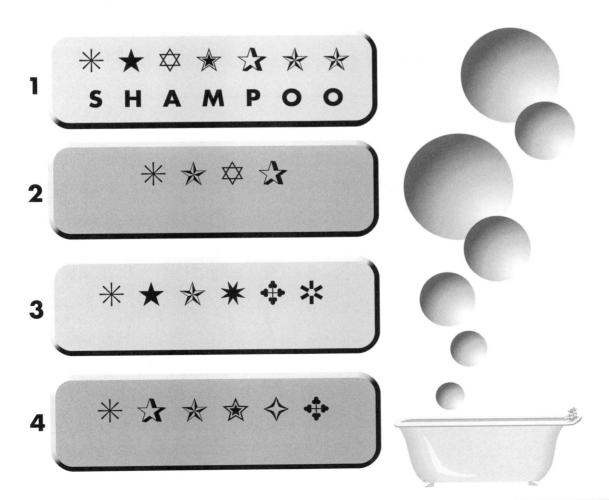

1 ✳ ★ ✡ ✭ ☆ ✩ ✦
  S H A M P O O

2

3

4

128. ON LINE

Add one line to complete each letter and spell out a real online word.

129. LINKS

Which word will go after the first word and before the second word?

BANANA(_ _ _ _)FLINT

130. FACE FACTS

Use the letters that
make up the face
to make a name.

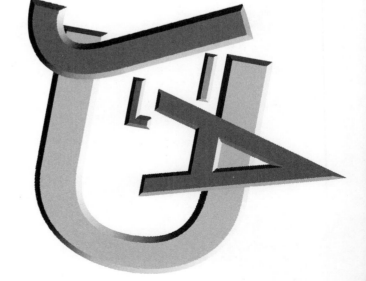

131. BACK WORDS

Solve the clues: the second answer is the first answer written backwards.

DIVIDE ∗ SNARE

_ _ _ _ ∗ _ _ _ _

132. 'ANDY ANDY!

In Andy Mann's workshop there's a shelf that is full of boxes of nails, nuts, bolts and screws.

He's just bought even more boxes! He's got 20 giant boxes of nails, 10 ordinary sized boxes of nails, 10 boxes of nuts and bolts, and 10 boxes of screws. The shelf is long enough to take 30 giant boxes of nails. The ordinary boxes of nails are half the size of the giant boxes, and they are the same size as the boxes of nuts and bolts and the boxes of screws.

How many of these new boxes can he fit onto the shelf in the workshop?

133. TOP TEN

complete the word by filling the spaces with a whole number between ONE and TEN.

1
6 4 **P R I S _ _ _ R** 2^5

134. NUMBER-RING

Move around the circle. You have to write a number in the blank section that will continue the number pattern.

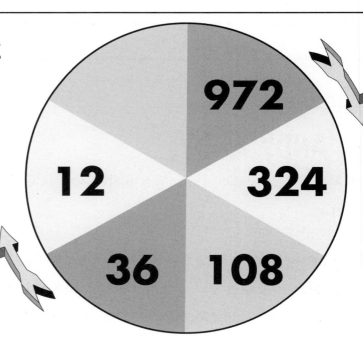

972
324
12
36 108

135. ADDER

Using other words with the same meaning, can you create a new word from two separate ones?

DECAY	— — —	
+ DINED	+ — — —	
= REVOLVE	= — — — — — —	

136. AFTER-WORDS

Which word can go after all these words to make new words?

F O X _____

G R E Y _____

W O L F _____

137. WORLD TOUR

Get travelling and find six different countries in the grid. Start at the letter in the top left square and move in any direction except diagonally. Every letter is used once.

B	R	A	E	N	M
W	S	Z	D	R	A
E	L	I	E	K	J
D	A	N	C	P	A
E	R	D	A	A	N
N	F	A	N	A	C

138. BADGER

Benita collects badges.

If she doubled the number that she has then she would have 99 more than if she halved her collection.

How many badges has
Benita collected?

139. SPLITZER

This row of ten letters can be split into two five-letter words which are the names of two animals that live in water. Words read from left to right and the letters are in the correct order. What are they?

S T H R A O R U T K

/
_____

140. FOOTPATH

Which path contains the most footprints?

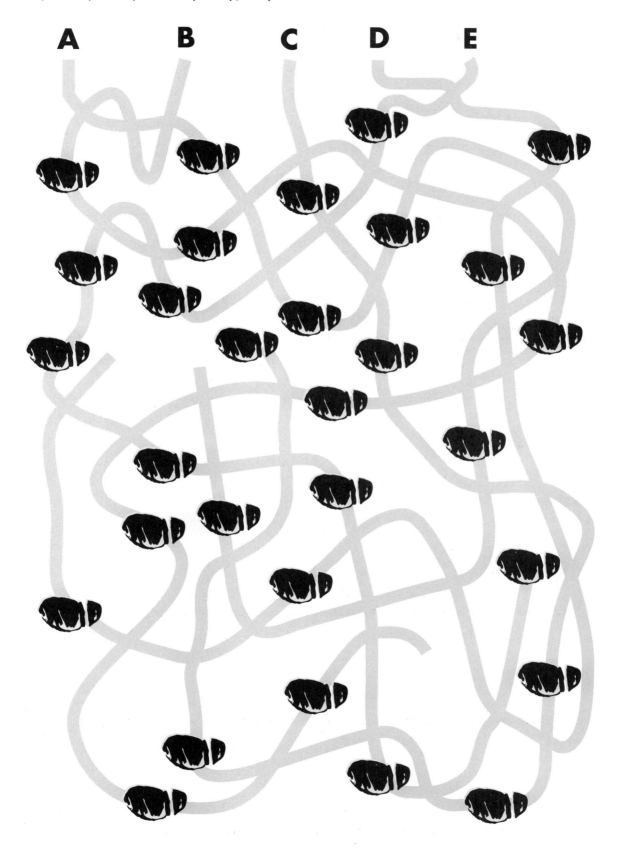

141. MIND THE GAP

Which single four-letter word completes all of the following words?

F E _ _ _ _

O I _ _ _ _ S S

D E C _ _ _ _ D

_ _ _ _ N

142. RIDDLER

Starting from the letter Z and working back through the alphabet, find three letters that name people that you're not friendly with!

143. SECRET SEVEN

Rearrange the letters in the word below to make another word of seven letters.

F R E T F U L

_ _ _ _ _ _ _

CLUE

Think
CHOCOLATE

144. SPLIT UP

The words below have been split in half and the ends moved round.
Can you repair the splits?

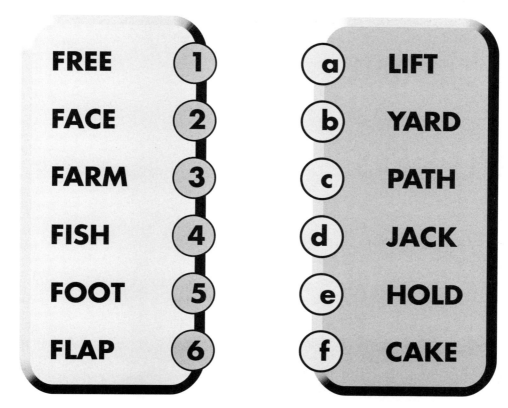

FREE	1		a	LIFT
FACE	2		b	YARD
FARM	3		c	PATH
FISH	4		d	JACK
FOOT	5		e	HOLD
FLAP	6		f	CAKE

LEVEL TWO ANSWERS

1. BEAM ME UP
It will take seven journeys.

1.   X and Z stay in zone A. You transport Y to zone B.

2.   You return from B to A on your own, leaving Y at B.

3.   Z stays in zone A. You transport X to zone B.

4.   You return from B to A bringing back Y, leaving X alone at B.

5.   Y is now left to stay in zone A. You transport Z to zone B.

6.   You return from B to A on your own, leaving Z and X together.

7.   You transport Y to zone B, to rejoin the others.
   (Bet you wish you never captured them now!)

2. MIND THE GAP
Log.

3. AFTER WORDS
Time.

4. FOLDED
Cube 4.

5. RED ALERT
Leave Tonight.

6. INSTRUMENTAL

1. Trumpet
2. Drum
3. Lute
4. Flute.

7. STRAIGHT AND CROOKED

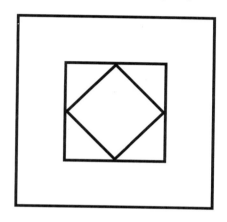

8. SAD START

9. SPLITZER

Ankle/Elbow.

10. TIME OUT

1. Hour
2. Year
3. Day
4. Month.

11. SPINNER

W	A	S	T	E
A	M	P	L	E
S	H	O	R	E
W	O	R	D	S
V	O	T	E	S

12. FIFTH DIMENSION

15	8	10	6	37	17
12	30	25	36	40	50
70	65	13	8	16	12
21	70	25	35	50	40
50	40	32	60	46	30
17	24	50	16	28	60

13. ADDER

War + Den = Warden.

14. SPACE TREK
only portal 2 logs on to a path to the planet.

15. SECRET SEVEN
outside.

16. TAKE OFF
Number 4.

17. BACK WORDS
Gums * Smug.

18. STACK SYSTEM
1. Chapel
2. Cheap
3. Cape
4. Cap
5. Clap
6. Place
7. Palace.

19. LINKS
Tennis.

20. VANISHING POINT
Ghost.

21. TRIANGLE TEST
13.

22. BACK NUMBERS

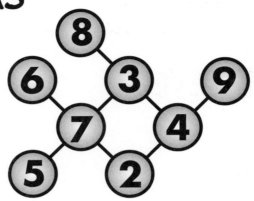

23. MORE OR LESS?

There are 49 days in seven weeks.

There are 48 spaces between the spokes.

24. COMPUTER CODE

Printer.

25. MIND THE GAP

Net.

26. SEEING DOUBLE

27. SQUARE SEARCH

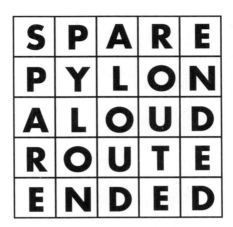

28. WHAT'S NEXT?

S. First letters of numbers. O for One, T for Two, T for Three, F for Four, F for Five, S for Six.

29. PYRAMID

30. FRUIT SPLIT

Tangerine is split between the words FELT ANGER IN EVERYONE'S.

31. TOP TEN

Ten. This completes the word listened.

32. TAKING SHAPE

Stars.

33. MIDDLE MOVES

1. fir for
2. Map Mop
3. Rig Rug
4. March Match
5. Leading Leaving.

34. SECRET SEVEN

Magenta.

35. CLOG-WORK!

4 and 6.

36. STRANGE SIGNS

Sign C. They are numbers shown with a mirror image. C shows number 5.

37. FACE FACTS

Victoria.

38. ADDER

Wit + Her = Wither.

39. AFTER-WORDS

Cake.

40. LINKS

Air.

41. NUMBER FIT

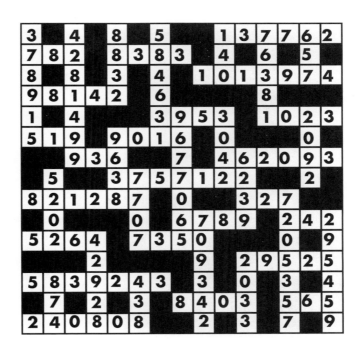

42. SPLITZER

Brake/Wheel.

43. BURIED TREASURE

Five hours.

44. BACK WORDS

Stop * Pots.

45. FEEDING TIME

46. NUMBER-RING

126. Add 21 each time.

47. SECRET SEVEN

Marines.

48. WHAT AM I?

Radio.

49. MIND THE GAP

Chip.

50. STARGAZER

1. Kilt 2. Knot 3. Pins 4. Snip 5. Plot 6. Soot.

51. MOSAIC

52. COLLECTORS

Dan. The number will always be an odd number.

53. BROTHERS AND SISTERS

1. Richard 2. Paul 3. Mark 4. David 5. Alice 6. Sally 7. Rebecca 8. Julie.
Brothers and sisters are: Richard and Sally, Paul and Alice, Mark and Julie, David and Rebecca.

54. TAKE SIDES

27 triangles have 81 sides, while both 20 squares and 16 pentagons have 80 sides.

55. ADDER

Off + End = offend.

56. LOST LANDS

1. China 2. Peru 3. France.

57. RING OF FIRE

1. Fire 2. File 3. Fill 4. Fall 5. Tall 6. Till 7. Tile 8. Tire.

58. REPEATER

1. Scar 2. Care 3. Area 4. Real.

59. ON LINE

Send.

60. TEN TIMES

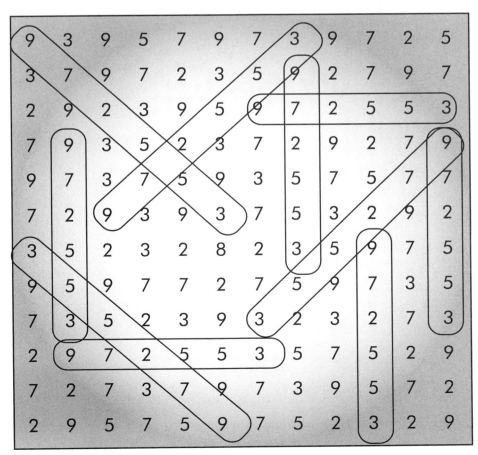

61. BACK WORDS

Flow * Wolf.

62. WHAT'S NEXT?

R. Letters are in alphabetical order, with two missed out at each move.

63. ANIMAL TRACKS

1. Camel 2. Lion 3. Leopard 4. Bear 5. Elephant 6. Tiger 7. Ape.

64. THE LAST STRAW

Glass A.

65. SECRET SEVEN

Kitchen.

66. BOWLING

There are six games.

67. STORMY WEATHER!

1. Fog 2. Storm 3. Thunder 4. Lightning.

68. TIME TOTAL

Both equal 96.

69. ODD ONE OUT

Actor. The other words are made out of the letters A, C, E, R and T.

70. SHOW TIME

30. There were only three ladies: a lady, her daughter, who was also the mother of the first lady's granddaughter. Two mothers, two daughters, three people!

71. AFTER WORDS

Life.

72. MIND THE GAP

Use.

73. HALF TIME

1. Also 2. Solo 3. Lobe 4. Best 5. Stab 6. Able 7. Leap.

74. BREAKERS

Marsh/Swamp.

75. DOMINOES

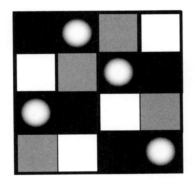

76. FACE FACTS

Josie.

77. FAIR AND SQUARE

Vein.

78. BODY LANGUAGE

1. 'Shin' to make sunshine 2. 'Arm' to make charming 3. 'Hair' to make Chairman.

79. WORKPLACE

1. Teacher 2. Diver 3. Minister 4. Salesmen.

80. NUMBER-RING

13. Half the number.

81. ADDER

Ten + Ant = Tenant.

82. HOW MANY?

Three. Numbers refer to the straight lines in the letters.

83. WHO'S THAT GIRL?

Melissa.

84. HAUNTED HOUSE

1. Dungeon 2. Cellar 3. Attic.

85. LINKS

Apple.

86. HALF CENTURY

Line B.

87. SPLITZER

Knife/Spoon.

88. SIGN PLEASE

880 - 400 = 480.

89. ON THE WILD SIDE

Panther.

90. TOP TEN
Two. This completes the word driftwood.

91. MIND THE GAP
Dot.

92. LINKS
Bank.

93. BACK WORDS
Pit * Tip.

94. LEAD ON!
Lead A.

95. SECRET SEVEN
Chalets.

96. S FOR STARTERS
Ten.

97. AFTER WORDS
Fire.

98. PASS NUMBER
54132.

99. FACE FACTS
Michael.

100. ALPHABET

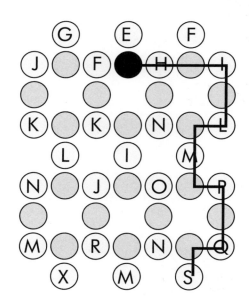

101. QUARTERBACK

102. SECRET SEVEN

Tornado.

103. MIND THE GAP

Text.

104. I-SPY

3. The words of the others are the same backwards and forwards.

105. DIVIDERS

9	32	7	8	12	9
3	2	9	9	13	3
15	9	3	18	19	9
7	6	21	5	24	4
6	13	27	18	3	6
9	8	20	16	13	12

106. AFTER-WORDS

Pipe.

107. FIRST CHANGE

1. Den Ten 2. Bed Red 3. Daft Raft 4. Gift Lift 5. Chick Thick.

108. HOW MANY?

14.

109. ADDER

Pal + Let = Pallet.

110. NUMBER-RING

51. Take away 12 each time.

111. SPLITZER

Brown/White.

112. ON GUARD

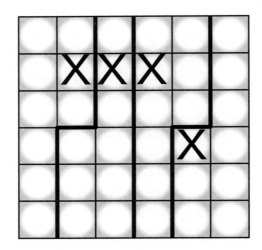

113. BACK WORDS

Edit * Tide.

114. WHAT'S NEXT?

K. Letters go backward through the alphabet, with two missed out at each move.

115. LIFT OFF

1. Wing 2. Nose 3. Engine.

116. NUMBER NAMES

ANITA = 12. T = 4. N = 3. A = 2. I = 1.

117. WHAT'S MISSING?

The letter E is missing. The finished sentence reads: There's something needed to complete the sentence.

118. RHYMER

Modem.

119. JUICY!

1. Orange 2. Lemon 3. Lime.

120. LUCKY NUMBERS

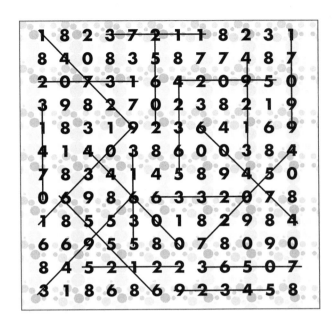

121. SECRET SEVEN

General.

122. LINE NINE

Rat, foe, nut – FORTUNATE

123. BALANCING ACT

Both are exactly the same length.

124. MEAL DEAL

Beth will pay 2. The initial letter of each name decides how much each lady pays.
Alice starting with the 1st letter of the alphabet pays 1,
Carol starting with the 3rd letter pays 3,
Donna starting with the fourth letter pays 4.

125. MIND THE GAP

Bit.

126. CAMOUFLAGE

Hyena.

127. BATH TIME

1. Shampoo
2. Soap
3. Shower
4. Sponge.

128. ON LINE

Internet.

129. LINKS

Skin.

130. FACE FACTS

Julia.

131. BACK WORDS
Part * Trap.

132. 'ANDY ANDY!

None. The shelf is already full.

133. TOP TEN
one. This completes the word prisoner.

134. NUMBER-RING
4. Divide by 3 at each move.

135. ADDER
Rot + Ate = Rotate.

136. AFTER WORDS
Hound.

137. WORLD TOUR
1. Brazil
2. Sweden
3. France
4. Denmark
5. Japan
6. Canada.

138. BADGER
She has 66 badges. Doubling the collection would give 132. Halving the collection would give 33.

139. SPLITZER
Shark/Trout.

140. FOOTPATH
Path E has most footprints. It contains eight.

141. MIND THE GAP
Line.

142. RIDDLER
The letters are N M E. They read as enemy!

143. SECRET SEVEN
Truffle.

144. SPLIT UP
1. e
2. a
3. b
4. f
5. c
6. d.